T5-AFB-446

# The Last Call of Mourning

# The Last Call of Mourning

CHARLES L. GRANT

DOUBLEDAY & COMPANY, INC.
GARDEN CITY, NEW YORK
1979

All of the characters in this book are fictitious, and
any resemblance to actual persons, living or dead, is purely
coincidental.

ISBN: 0-385-14376-1
Library of Congress Catalog Card Number 78-20075
Copyright © 1979 by Charles L. Grant
All Rights Reserved
Printed in the United States of America
*First Edition*

## AUTHOR'S DEDICATION

*For temperature days and quiet suite nights,*
*And knowing why Alpha will never touch ground;*
*For a street named Hawthorne*
*And a tapestry called Parric—*
    *For David, my mentor*
    *And David, my friend.*

# The Last Call of Mourning

# ONE

A favorite place, a secret place, a world not bonded to grownups and growing: a veiled gap in a man-tall hedge, or a ten-plank tree house with rope ladders and codes, or the dark corner of an unfinished cellar behind the always warm bulk of a begrimed and sturdy furnace that purrs like a beast at home on the veldt. In the spring, wherever they are, they whisper promises of loving full moons and daring raids and living dolls and flashing steel that pricks no blood; in summer, wherever they are, they spawn pirates and ballerinas and quarterbacks and dragonriders, heros and heroines with no thought of dying. And in November they are refuge, retreats, invulnerable barriers against the air that turns damp, the colors that shade grey, and the twilight that hovers between autumn and winter when the sun dies before supper and is reborn before waking . . . and the promise of soft cleansing snow is a falsehood grimly denounced when the streets turn black with yet another shower.

In Oxrun Station it was no different; and Cyd Yarrow in her darkmood wished for a moment that it could have been.

It was a lot easier back then, she thought, unwilling for a while to release the oddly comforting gloom. A lot easier when she was called Cindy. When her hair was still blonde without that tantalizing hint of strawberry, and she wore with what she'd hoped was a brave soldier's grin the gleaming silver-blue of a fence of braces and doused her face each night, each morning, with concoctions the ads said would keep her skin clear and the boys flocking round; when a football game was plaid blankets and groping and rising with every touchdown to scream so hard that throats were raw, could barely manage a laugh. When love was muted hues and distant violins and races across a meadow and huddling in a rain-splattered car and a boy/man grabs you by the shoulders in the middle of the street and kisses you and you don't care and kiss him right back.

Today, however, she felt as though she were attending a funeral.

A funeral whose centerpiece she almost thought she knew.

Her umbrella was black, raincoat black (despite the silvered buttons and red-wool lining), even the boots that hugged her slender legs to the thigh were black. She wore little make-up, and the eyes that someone once had called a soft porcelain blue were hard now and seemed ready to crack at the first tear. Her hair, long ago a cloud that settled on her shoulders, curled just slightly enough to give at her nape the illusion of length, swept left to right across her forehead to hide a faint widow's peak. Around it was a silk kerchief hastily tied beneath a chin barely rounded. Hastily tied, silk, and black.

She'd left the house immediately after lunch and had walked quickly, directly across the broad lawn into the trees that mustered at the rear. Elms. Oaks. One curious cage of white birch and a rough-barked pine. The undergrowth had been kept reasonably clear, and it was an easy hundred yards to a fast-crumbling wall that, when she was younger, was star-tall and heroic, now ancient and feeble; and she thought more than sadly that all she need do would be to give it a shove and it would fall in slow motion outward into the forest that climbed the Station's surrounding hills. She hadn't been here in years, but she'd found the place without trying; and for the first time since waking a smile found her lips and coaxed them to part.

A favorite place. A secret place.

A small, unelegant shack her brothers Evan and Rob had built from loose fieldstone and plywood. It had been their fortress, castle, dungeon, clubhouse, complete with a secret exit that led through the wall and seldom worked after rain bulged the wood. And when they were done and decided they hated it, they gave it to her with appropriate solemn ceremony. Here, then, she dreamed of traveling, of marrying, of loving, of princes and kings and fantasy wizards, sitting on the hardened dirt floor to entertain spiders and ants and a stray fly or rambling hornet. And once, she recalled as her smile grew wider, a praying mantis had perched on the threshold and stared at her for nearly ten minutes. It had terrified her, then calmed her; and once she dared blink and shift, it was gone . . . and she liked to imagine it had left under cover of a pale green fire.

A sudden gust dropped rain and dead leaves around her. She shivered, reached over and tried to open the latched door. It screamed wooden protest, gave an inch, gave another, and when a spider rushed out she started and leapt back, then laughed at herself.

"The famous world traveler undone by a bug," she said, one hand lightly touching the shack's canted top.

One month ago, almost to the day, she'd returned to Oxrun from a trip her father had sponsored, refusing to allow her to touch her own savings. He told her that in decades past it was called the Grand Tour, a leisurely sweep through Europe, sampling the languages and the food and the rigors of first-class living. But now, staring at her childhood huddling in the rain, she remembered little about it. The grassy beaches at Lausanne, the incredible traffic in Rome, the melancholy of scum-covered canals in Amsterdam . . . too many images, too much excitement.

When she came home, she'd been breathless. Bubbling. Dozens of rolls of film aching to be developed.

A month later she was bored.

In Oxrun Station there was no Louvre or National Gallery, neither Sacre Coeur nor windmill profusion. Here, the Chancellor Inn and the Mariner Cove were the nightspots for the young, special dinners for the family; the community college with occasional film festivals, the library and its readings, the churches their fairs, the park its games when the weather was fine.

Cyd shook her head slowly, wondering how she'd stood it all these years without screaming, without ranting, without scrambling for escape.

She scolded herself then, knowing it was her flair for the utterly melodramatic that had tainted the November gloom with an overlay of her own. Post-Thanksgiving let-down. Perhaps, she thought; yet it didn't stop her wishing, just for a moment, that there was something more to the village than a shrouded, untraceable history.

Another gust, stronger, and the umbrella was nearly torn

from her hands. She braced herself until the wind died. Another glance at the shack, and she turned to make her way back. Stopped and stared at the house bulked before her.

Sighed.

The older she grew the smaller it became.

Now merely an oversized house, once it had been a massive block of Georgian brick-and-marble with, on this side, iron-railed balconies for the three second-story bedrooms (her brothers' on the corners and hers in the center); and below, a house-long patio of flagstone and slate surrounded by a low, sculptured brick wall with planters at intervals where nothing seemed to grow no matter how her mother tried. On her left, below Evan's rooms, a trio of wide windows to mark the country kitchen; in the center a wide glass entryway opening to the main hall; and on the right french doors that set off the library—a cavern of books and periodicals she'd been unable to touch until she'd picked up her degree and her father thought her ready.

And between the trees and the house, two acres of what Evan once called the family's virgin plot—no flowers, no fountains, no topiary . . . just grass. Over *there* was croquet when the aunts and uncles came, and *there* touch football, and *there* vicious badminton. It should have been English, she thought, and Victorian, and the women should have had parasols and the men unruffled grey coats.

Now she was older, and now it was so . . . small.

God, she wondered, how did I stand it?

She was ready to return to the shack and her past, when the hall door swung open and Evan stepped outside, waving to her frantically. She almost waved back, hesitated when his hands grew to fists, then ran across the rain-soaked yard. Frowning, but not worried. Darting through one of the gaps in the patio wall while she struggled to fold the umbrella, failed and tossed it angrily aside. By the time she'd reached the door, Evan had taken her arm and was pulling her down the hardwood floor toward the front.

"She's done it again," he said, gasping, his lean face more pale than usual, his curly black hair plastered wetly against his forehead as though he too had been outside.

"What's she done now?" she said, taking back her arm with a yank.

"What does Mother usually do?" he said. "She's fallen again."

"Oh, God," she said, more wearily than anxiously. "What now, painting a ceiling?"

"Papering the nursery."

"Great. Just great. Not a kid in this place for a million years, and she has to paper the stupid nursery."

Evan said nothing, only raced to the second floor.

The house was cored by a squared-spiral staircase carpeted a deep and soft brown, bannister and posts waxed and mirror bright. The landing itself extended into a corridor that led left and right to the rear bedroom suites, became a double-sized hallway that swept toward the front. Along all these stretches paneling reached to the ceiling without being broken by portraits or prints; a light knotted pine that despite faint dust gleamed like glass from a century of cleaning. Gaslight and amber globes now flickering electricity. Carved wooden sconces and pale white tapers that seldom were used despite power failures and storms.

A muttering.

Cyd slowed, and stopped at the corner. On the left were the closed dark doors of her father's rooms, on the far right the newly white paint that marked her mother's. In a decorative alcove that stretched straight ahead for less than ten feet an oval stained-glass window of peacocks and doves where, as a child, she'd tried for a harlequin tan.

And between the alcove and her mother's rooms the family nursery.

Evan had already gone inside, and Rob was standing stolidly at the open door. He was Evan's opposite in temperament and color, but just as handsome, just as tall, with most of his weight impressively in his chest. When he saw her he stepped back a pace right away, his tongue licking at his lips, his eyes squinting behind gold-rimmed wire glasses. He shrugged when her brows rose in silent question, pointed, and she moved past him to stand at the threshold.

The room was smaller than it appeared from the hall, its toys long since jammed into two large closets, a rocking horse cocked precariously on end in a far corner, a cedar storage chest beneath one of the curtained windows. The floor was littered with dropcloths and newsprint, strips and balls of Mother Goose wallpaper yellowed and stiff. She counted four red plastic buckets of warm water, a paste brush, half a dozen wastebaskets overflowing and shoved aside, and two paste containers open and drying. A short stepladder had been propped against the right-hand wall, and at its foot lay her mother. She was groaning softly and, at the same time, resisting Evan's efforts to slide a hand behind her back to help her sit up.

"For crying out loud, I'm not dead," she snapped at him in a voice that made sandpaper seem remarkably like velvet. She glared at him, glanced up and saw Cyd for the first time. "Cynthia, will you tell him I'm not—" She groaned again, slapped once more at his hand and pushed at him until he sat back on his heels. Then, sighing and using her elbows awkwardly, she struggled to sit up, took a deep breath and sniffed as though searching for a foul odor to be damned.

Her hair, an unashamed cloudgrey, was dotted with bits of plaster and paste and a few curling strands of brightly colored paper. Her face was the same, and the smock she wore carried medals of all the rooms she'd done herself, every shade, every design. It was, she often claimed, nearly as old as she was herself. Her lips were as thick as Rob's, and brighter; her eyes as blue as Cyd's, and softer. Only a faint delicate webbing about her mouth and blunted nose and carefully screened temples betrayed her to the fifty-five years she had already weathered.

"Mother," Evan protested in obvious resignation, "you could have broken your back."

"I didn't, though, did I?" she said, grabbing his shoulder and hauling herself to her feet, brushing carefully at her smock and the plain slacks bagging at the knees. Cyd took a quick step forward, frowning, worried, but only Rob had the foresight to ask her what happened.

Myrtle Yarrow shrugged. "I was on that idiot ladder, see—that confounded paper must be older than your father—and I reached out to yank down a strip and my foot slipped." She glanced at the floor-worn slippers on her feet, shook one experimentally and nodded. "No grip anymore, you see. I fell, that's all."

"But you landed on your back," said Evan sternly.

"Yes," she said, nodding again. "Yes, as a matter of fact I did. And no worse for the wear, I'll tell you. Now what's the matter with all of you?" she demanded abruptly. "I'm not in my grave yet, you know. Honestly, you'd think I was—"

"Mother," Rob said quietly, "you should be careful."

She blinked once, slowly, before putting her hands on her hips and glaring at them all. Then she took Evan's arm and led him back to the hallway. "I need a drink," she announced to her sons. "You boys will join me. Cyd," she said over her shoulder, "would you mind running to Bradford's? I have a bracelet waiting. For the party tomorrow."

"Another one?"

"Don't know what happened to the last one," Myrtle said blithely. "Must have lost it, I guess." She frowned, broke it and grinned as Evan moved her toward the stairs. "Must be getting old, my dear, must be getting old. Please don't forget, will you?"

"But Mother . . ."

Cyd stopped herself, content with just nodding. Evan's diamond ring, Rob's diamond stickpin, her father's . . . she scowled as she tried to remember, then shrugged and gave it up. It was as though there were a jinx against jewelry in the house, with her mother the worst victim . . . or the most absentminded offender.

She heard their footsteps fading, their voices softening, and began a slow wandering around the room. Looking at the dying paper, the mottled walls, kicking once at the stack of new rolls behind the door. From the look of it, her mother was working wherever the old paper gave her the least trouble, and it reminded her too much of some ancient forgotten relic. Absently, she righted one of the buckets, scuffed idly at the debris and stood in front of the ladder. She grabbed its sides and shook it to test for stability. It did not move, and when she checked she could see nothing on any of the steps that might have been slippery. She sighed at her mother's incredible luck, left the room and closed the door behind her, her hands deep in the raincoat's pockets as she made her way back downstairs and across the slate foyer to the front door.

On her right was the living room, more used now than when she was a child; and on her left a massive room that took up that entire half of the house. Her father called it the sitting room, where guests had to be entertained before dining and parties were held when there was no dancing. It was paneled, like the living room, in walnut from floor to ceiling, the inner wall split by two fieldstone fireplaces that in turn were separated by ceiling-tall doors that led to the dining room. And save for the oriental throws scattered across pegged pine, the entire area was decorated in browns and soft golds. It could have been a cold place where formality reigned, but her mother had seen to it early on that warm instead was its keynote and code.

At the moment Myrtle was stretched out on a slightly curved couch that faced the near hearth, her right arm trailing along the carved-wood back. She seemed to be suffering no ill effects from the fall, but Cyd thought one of her brothers ought to be calling Doctor Foster. That, however, would have to wait, she noted with a wry grin—now they were standing before her, their hands clasped behind their backs and looking for all the world like schoolboys trapped placing a snake in Mother's desk.

She called out softly, waved though she knew they would pay her no mind, and buttoned her raincoat absently as she stepped outside.

Despite its pretentions to size, the front of the house was weathered plain and unimposing. It faced a circular drive that enclosed the only garden her mother permitted, narrowing to a blacktopped lane that darted almost fearfully under a canopy of elm toward the Williamston Pike. A generation earlier spotlights had illuminated facade and flowers from sunset to midnight; now the only light came dimly from within, as if the glow had retreated from the grasp of the trees.

Cyd rubbed a thoughtful finger along the smooth line of her nose and jumped the four low steps of the half-moon porch to the cracked concrete walk that led along the outside of the circle to what had once been a row of stables, off the house's left side. The building was wooden, low and flat-roofed and badly in need of another coat of white. Where the stalls had been were five broad doors, one for each of them, hers on the far end where the trees blocked the bulk of the perimeter wall.

Her car.

A blue four-door sedan Father had complained she drove like a fury when the police weren't around and she was on her own. Skybright when new, now it was faded from hood to trunk, sporting signs of spreading rust along the door rims and pitted chrome bumpers. When, not long before she'd left for England, her father had none-too-subtly suggested she trade it in for something . . . nicer . . . she had cried all night and slept on the back seat.

Gently she kicked in a ritual all the tires in turn, and sighed with a grin at the hubcaps dented and unmatching.

She loved it, babied it, had once decided that her life since graduation was so tied up with it that, when it died, she would too.

After closing and locking the garage door behind her, then, and slipping back behind the wheel, she glanced over at the house, frowning slightly, wondering if perhaps she shouldn't call Doc Foster on her own, or drop in at his Centre Street office. And immediately she thought it, she dismissed it. Since the night Barton Yarrow had almost been lost through clumsy surgery for what was supposed to have been a routine extraction of a benign larynx tumor, her mother had sworn off most doctors on a hastily implemented principle. And when no one complained, home remedies became the rule as if they had always been.

Still, the fall . . .

Forget it, she told herself; you've enough to worry about as it is.

Slowly she drove down the lane, turned west onto the Pike and headed for the village.

The road here was narrow—two miles from the Station's center —had once been a carriage route leading to the estates belonging to Oxrun's founders. But though the road and its name remained, the estates were dwindling rapidly, for the most part sliced into smaller parcels on demand of higher taxes and a lifestyle dying. The division was still there, however: the area "beyond the park" and the town itself; a division Cyd thought foolish, and somewhat embarrassing.

The rain stopped.

The only sound the beat of the windshield wipers thumping. On the left began the village park behind its black iron fencing as the road rose and fell over a low ancient hill. And once crested, she blinked at the lights that marked Oxrun Station. As many times as she had driven this way, she was never prepared for the sudden appearance of the town, as though a dark grey veil had been abruptly yanked from her eyes. She snapped on her running lights and took the second left turn onto Centre Street, barely noticing the library on the corner, paying more attention to the three blocks ahead of her—the town's only business street, the hub of daily living. Here were the shops, the luncheonette, the banks and the lawyers, brokerage firms, doctors . . . sure signs, she thought, that the Station was different, reasonably wealthy and reasonably content. Those who did not live beyond the park lived here in the village itself in Victorians and New England Colonials and offsprings of both.

Quietly. Peacefully. Aware of the world, and keeping it distant.

Between High Street and Steuben, then, she pulled into a vacant space at the curb, switched off the ignition and rolled down the window. She twisted to rest her arms on the door, her chin tucked into an elbow as her gaze swept in from the corner, from The Smoke Shop, Anderson's Shoes, The Melody Shop, Bartlett's Toys to . . . a dark-faced store whose plate-glass windows had been carefully frosted so no one could see inside.

Cyd grinned.

A favorite place. Her secret place soon to be baptized.

A pleasantly soft sigh, and she gathered up her purse, hung the strap over her shoulder and opened the door. Slipped out. Closed the door with a push of her hip and sidled until she was leaning back against the front fender. Kicked back with one boot and struck the hubcap gently. A car passed and sprayed her, but she scarcely noticed.

A favorite place.

A secret place.

Her smile shattered suddenly when she looked up, looked left, saw a huge grey limousine bearing down on her rapidly, its side barely clearing the other parked cars. From somewhere behind her a woman screamed. From somewhere inside her an order screamed, but she could not move. And could not look away—from the teeth of the chromed grille or the windshield's blind face that reflected the streetlamps in kaleidoscopic nightmare.

She had half turned to run when two hands suddenly gripped her shoulders, lifted her up and back and across the hood.

The limousine streaked on without slowing down, took the first corner shrieking, was gone, and it was silent.

Slowly, then, she was helped to the sidewalk where she grabbed at the man's arms to steady herself before shaking loose and slumping against her car.

"You know something," he said, his hands loose on his hips, "if that had been me, it would have been a beer truck, and it would have hit me."

"Luck of the Yarrows," she said, trying to grin, trying not to give way to the trembling inside her. "Ed Grange, damnit, if I didn't know better I'd swear you set that up."

"You're welcome," he said with a half-smile. "Any time."

He was not much taller than she, and not much heavier; but his face was far less velvet, much more stone. Myrtle called it a rugged sort of handsome; Cyd called it uninspired. His nose was too large, his chin too perfectly squared, his cheekbones too high, his hair too blond . . . and the smile widening to a grin was too arrogant by far. She would have said more, but her legs abruptly refused to hold her any longer, and she did not protest when he took her arm and stared at her with black eyes narrowed with concern.

"Trust me," she said. "I won't die on you."

Several pedestrians had passed nearby, and Ed turned to them and waved them away with a professional smile. They moved, reluctantly, their heads a degree behind the direction of their feet.

Cyd, fighting a conflict of nausea and dizziness, barely resisted the urge to stick out her tongue.

"The cops," he said then, not really a question.

"No, I don't think so. It's too late, he's gone."

"Well . . . don't you think you at least owe me a drink?"

She wiped a hand over her face, tugged at the handbag's strap and stood away from the car. "Is that what knights are getting these days?"

Ed shrugged. Then stared at her in frank admiration. "I think, if that had been me, I'd be on the ground in a puddle waiting for a doc."

"I told you," she said, taking his arm. "The luck of the Yarrows."

"You sure you're all right?"

"Edwin Grange, stop fussing!"

"I'll stop fussing when you stop pretending."

She looked back at her car, saw in a moment she could not stop her body trapped between her car and the Greybeast, spun around and dropped, discarded like a doll.

"You said," she muttered weakly, "something about a drink?"

# TWO

Diagonally opposite the Chancellor Avenue police station was the Mariner Cove, a low and long Montecello miniature less than a year old, windowless (for mystery) and signless (for confidence). The only interruptions in the clean brick front were two white double-doors; the one led to a dining room specializing in seafood, the other to a lounge heavily dark in mahogany and ebony, with carriage lamps on thick squared posts, exposed beams, and nightwine walls that felt remarkably like velvet to the touch. There was no music, no filtering of chatter from the adjoining restaurant, no flirtations with the waitresses or gambling with the bartender. Church-quiet. Relaxing. An island within an island for some to shed their tensions by sighing instead of screaming.

The bar was in the center, surrounded by small pine tables and captain's chairs, in turn surrounded by a string of low-backed booths whose faces were artfully screened by draped fish netting. Red chimneys and candles. No tiers of bottles to distort the curved mirror as the bartender and his shadow moved swiftly, soundlessly, on a burgundy carpet.

Immediately they entered, Ed led her to a table hidden on the far side of the bar, beneath a narrow print of the USS *Constitution*. He waited until she sat, lifted the raincoat from her shoulders and draped it over the rounded back of her chair. Then, with a shrug, he was out of his own beige topcoat and facing her over the chimney, the brass stand, and the unlighted candle. He glanced around the near empty room, then back to her.

"Down among the peasants," he said with a smile.

"Don't knock those peasants, sir," she said. "They keep the ladies alive."

"Barely, Cyd," he said quietly. "Good Lord, what were you

thinking of? No," he added before she could answer, "where were you, is a better question. Because you sure weren't there."

The room darkened briefly, and she ran a hand through her hair before patting it unnecessarily. "I . . ." She swallowed at the bile rising, nodded weakly when Ed offered to order for them. And when the waitress, in a nautical costume complete with tiny cap, smiled at them and left, she gripped the table's edge tightly. "I could have been killed."

Ed nodded, said nothing.

"My God, I could have been killed!"

And something denied it. People die; Yarrows don't. It was an axiom she had dedicated herself to since the death of her grandparents when she was less than five. But now . . . she cupped her hands around a glass the waitress placed before her, fought to find some warmth in the dark red wine within, her arms beneath the smooth cashmere sweater, the tightening at the back of her neck when, in her mind's eye, she saw the Greybeast again.

And where had she been? That was simple enough. Perhaps too simple for the state she was in.

The Station Bookmart had long been out of business, not for lack of readers but because its owners had decided Florida's Decembers were more conducive to long life than the bleak weak star that lightened Connecticut's winters. A jeweler had tried his luck there and couldn't compete with the others on the street; a lawyer tried it and didn't like the ambiance; and a toy store attempted a direct assault on Bartlett's, only to find that Dale Bartlett Blake was more than a match for an ambitious outsider. The shop had remained empty for nearly a month before, without warning, a grizzled workman in blue coveralls opened the door and hauled in all manner of carpentry equipment. Immediately after, he frosted the insides of the two narrow display windows, and several times a day since then someone would stand on the sidewalk and stare, trying to pierce the white fog and secondguess the new owner.

"Hey, Cyd," Ed whispered. "Are you all right?"

Her answering grin was weak, growing stronger, as she heard behind her the room filling with customers preparing a libation for the day-to-day gods that kept them afloat. She was glad her back was to the room. There was enough talk in the Station these days about the company she kept, gossip that had twice caused a fierce row with her parents. Not, she thought in soft silent scolding, that Ed Grange was poor company. Only . . . unexpected. The Yarrows, after all, were from beyond the park; and Ed was the owner of a firm that specialized in security work—providing guards and part-time patrolmen for those functions the Station's own limited force was unable to man adequately without skimping somewhere else. Ed himself was an ex-Station cop, and as such there was no animosity or professional rivalry between himself and Abe Stockton, the Chief of Police. The need was recognized, and pride in one meant pride in the other.

"Cyd, I think I'm coming down with the Plague."

She nodded absently. Staring at him, not seeing him. It was no secret that he loved her—at least not to her—and in the beginning she'd thought it a compliment to what she hoped was her fine humor and a caring about herself without the taint of vanity. But as for reciprocation . . . not, she thought, until she had worked out some proofs for her being.

She never supped with him, then, or walked with him through the park or along the streets; but he always managed to be at the house when there were too many dowagers with too many jewels, or checking the guards who patrolled the estates at night when she stepped out alone for a stroll along the Pike. Before Europe there had been those arguments with her parents, and since then . . . she frowned in abrupt realization—her mother suddenly didn't seem to care, and her father said nothing beyond a faint scowl whenever he happened to see them talking.

"Cyd, there's a purple scorpion in your hair. I think he's looking for a vacancy."

"Yarrow's Yard," she said, as though through a dream.

"What?"

"Yarrow's Yesterday's, maybe."

"Cyd, maybe I ought to get you a doctor, huh? Maybe I grabbed you too hard. Did you hit your head when—"

"Oh, sit down, Ed! You're making a scene." He froze at her words and lowered himself slowly. "Good," she said. "That's better."

He grunted, sipped at his drink and grimaced. "God," he said.

"Not enough blood, too much Mary." And he caught the waitress' elbow to ask for a glass of tomato juice.

"You're getting soft," she told him. "I remember the day you took a whole—what was it, a fifth of vodka?—and downed it without stopping."

"You'll also remember that I threw up and passed out."

"In Mother's garden no less. Her roses to be exact. I thought she would go through the roof." She laughed lightly, took some of her wine and let the warmth slide and ease the faint trembling. Then she stared at him, appraising. "You need a new suit," she decided. "Brown becomes you better than that blue thing."

He looked down at his chest, brushing at his lapels and running a palm along the length of his knit tie. "It serves. I must be inconspicuous, you know."

"You'd be more inconspicuous naked."

His eyebrows lifted. "You know about such things?"

Her sigh was jaded. "Europe had nothing better, I'm afraid," she said, setting an invisible monocle to her right eye. "It was frightfully difficult in Venice, however. The gondola rocking and all that. And I damn near fell out of the Tower of Pisa." She grinned, softened it when she saw she was teasing too much, that Ed for all his graces never understood when she was pulling his leg. "Ed," she said after a deliberate pause, "thank you. Really. I—"

"Hey, listen," he interrupted, not unkindly, "it's almost five and I have to get going. There's a charity fair at the high school tonight, and what with Thanksgiving vacation and all, the college crowd is going to be looking for some action."

"Did you have a good meal yesterday?"

He blinked rapidly, unsure, off-guard. "I went over to Harley to see my sister. Ate too much turkey, as usual."

"And now you're going into action. What action? The only action around this place is watching the beasts get ready for winter."

He rose and slipped into his coat, belted it and stood by her side until it was evident she wasn't going to join him. "You're too hard on the place, Cyd. And after today I would think you'd had enough action to last you a year."

*The Greybeast bearing down . . . windshield glaring the last of the sun . . . a face, a wavering shadow behind the wheel . . .*

"The least he could have done was stop," she said over her glass.

"He was probably drunk and too scared when he saw what he'd done. I'll ask around."

"Thanks," she said. "Meanwhile, if you don't mind, I'm going to stay right here for a while and count my blessings. See you at the party tomorrow? I guess Evan's called you already."

He grinned as he buttoned his coat to the neck. "Maybe. I'll have to check the bank to see how many safe deposit boxes were called for today."

She shook her head. "It's not that kind of thing this time. Lots of people, no fancies. Dad's on a new kick this year."

"Ah, the peasants again."

The word had no sting, but she felt it anyway, her smile tightening for a fraction of a second before she nodded and he left, one hand brushing over the round of her shoulder. A moment later her own hand reached up to touch it, softly, return to cup the glass. If she had known she was going to see Ed, she wouldn't have worn the cashmere—it clung too softly, revealing without exposing, and there was nothing she needed less now than Ed's friendship turning hungry. The peasants, she thought with a silent laugh. They had been kidding each other about peasants and Lords since the day they'd met nearly three years before; and at the time she'd taken umbrage, thinking him some sort of reverse snob before she understood there was no covetousness there . . . only a trace of wistful envy bound in realistic resignation. And in thinking about it she amazed herself in realizing that this, too, was part of Oxrun's existence—the rich, and the middle class, and an unspoken rule that no lines were ever to be drawn. Those who did—on either side of the fence—were soon enough ostracized to practice their snobbery, or martyrdom, elsewhere.

Which explained, in part, her own excitement now, and glad for her mother's excuse to get out of the house.

The store.

Yarrow's Yesterdays, or Yarrow's Yard, or Yarrow's *anydamnthing* was going to be hers.

Excuse.

She slapped a hand on the table, remembering her errand. She checked her watch and saw with a frown that Bradford's would already be closed. Not that it made any difference. Her mother could just as easily wait until morning, then fetch the bracelet herself.

If only she wouldn't keep losing the fool things!

Another glass of wine. Gazing blindly at the wallprint. Trying still to shake off the shroud of discontent that had settled over her more strongly when she'd visited the shack that afternoon. The Greybeast had already faded to a macabre joke she would tell her brothers with appropriate gestures and histrionic interpretation; but now she was back in the gloom November had fed her. And she knew what it was. She knew, and she wondered, and hoped there was a cure.

It wasn't Europe; she had traveled before.

It wasn't Ed; she'd had lovers near and distant before, too.

But she was the only girl of three, and her father had not wanted her. He loved her, to be sure, and protected her as fiercely as anyone had done—but there were still those occasional glances, those sideways looks when he thought she wasn't watching. It had been plain enough he wanted no part of her growing; it confused him because she'd taken her mother's role, accepting his yelling and his threats with patient, knowing smiles. She suspected he was trying to bring to life the blustering patriarch of Clarance Day's novel—be harsh outside and marshmallow in, all in orchestration of paternal love. The trouble with Barton Yarrow's interpretation was, Cynthia had begun to believe in the outside, not the in.

She stared at her glass.

You, she told herself, are starting to feel sorry, aren't you?

She nodded.

Then you're an idiot.

A momentary hush in the lounge made her stiffen, holding her glass halfway to her lips. Less than a moment, less than a second, but she felt it nevertheless and was not surprised when a shadow drifted over her table.

"Father," she said without looking up, "you're supposed to be home. You're late for supper, if you haven't missed it already."

He was well over six feet tall and a match for his sons in keeping himself fit. His hair was a carefully considered wash of white that looked down over his ears and brushed at the collar of his three-piece tweed suit. His face was flushed, as always, and the walrus mustache quivered as he sought for a word to keep his daughter in her place. She forestalled him, however, by rising and kissing him solidly on the cheek, waiting until he'd sat before taking her chair again.

"I don't suppose this is coincidence," she said, once again intent on the print above her head.

He shook his head, pulled a thick envelope out of his jacket pocket. "I met that man, Grange, on the street. He told me you were here." When she said nothing, he slid the envelope in front of her. "I've just come from Angus. He told me . . . well, damnit, Cyd, what are you trying to prove?"

"He wasn't supposed to say anything," she whispered, though not contritely. "He's got a bigger mouth than Rob."

"Your brother has nothing to do with this, I hope."

"Father, please keep your voice down."

Yarrow seemed to shrink within the greatcoat that matched his suit, but his expression remained stern as he dismissed the hovering waitress.

"And no, Rob had nothing to do with this. Or Evan. Or Mother. No one was supposed to know."

"*Fait accompli*, is that it?"

She shrugged. Something was wrong.

"My dear, I don't know what to say."

She shrugged again, and cursed herself for not getting another lawyer to handle the sale and transfer of title. But Angus Stone had been her family's protector since, it seemed, the day he'd stolen all Harvard's honors, and it was only natural she should go to him when the itch she'd discovered had to be scratched.

And when the silence became a near physical pain, she took a deep breath and let it out slowly. "I wanted something to do. It's as simple as that."

"Well, why the . . . why didn't you tell me?"

She tried not to frown. Why wasn't he bellowing?

"Because," she said, "I'm not a lawyer like Evan, and I hate banking—which is your and Rob's cross, not mine—and I refuse to wallpaper or paint in any fashion, shape or form, or redecorate a single room in a house that's too bloody big for us anyway."

"Your mother's good at it."

"Of course she is, but that's not the point."

"I know," he said surprisingly, and so quietly that she almost didn't hear him. "But you're . . . you're not the same since you came back, Cynthia, not the same at all."

"For all that, neither are you," she said without thinking, and leaned quickly back from the expression on his face. It had no name. Just a look. A look that as much slapped her and left a rising welt.

"All right," he said as though a decision had been made, "if this is what you want. You know, though, there's been a thousand movies made of this: rich girl, bored, tries quaint shop of her own, rich father opposes but secretly helps her, she's a success in spite of him and marries the poor boy and they live happily ever after. A thousand films. It's all very . . . B-movie, Cyd."

She could not help it; she gaped. "B-movie? Father, I didn't know you knew what that meant?"

He very nearly laughed, coughed instead. "You think I've been living in a vacuum all my life, girl? God Almighty. Anyway," and he tapped the envelope, "Angus wanted me to give you these."

"The creep," she muttered.

He laughed loudly and rose, put a hard hand on her shoulder. "It's all yours now, girl. I hope you know what you're doing."

"I don't know, Father," she said candidly. "I really don't."

He stiffened to say something, and she prayed he wouldn't. She couldn't stand a platitude now, and knew he was going to give her one. A platitude, a homily, some deathless fatherly advice that would cling burrlike to her forever. And when he didn't, when he only patted her shoulder gently and left, she could only twist to watch him, turning back when she saw several faces looking at her curiously.

He's tired, she thought in puzzled explanation for his generous behavior. A long day in the city buying banks and selling countries. Or perhaps it was a long-term after-effect of his stay at the Clinic. Each of her family, while she'd been in Europe, had been forced during bouts of serious illnesses to take a bed at the Kraylin Clinic out in the valley. No more than two or three days at the most, but each homecoming necessitated a day or two extra in bed. Only her father seemed not to have shaken off the pneumonia's debilitation; and considering her mother's new-found aversion to medicine, it was a wonder he had gone there at all, much less stayed.

She emptied her glass in a swallow, deciding it was too late and too useless for puzzling. And though she knew she should have felt at least a modicum of elation at her father's acquiescence, there was only a sensation, a premonition, that she hadn't had the last word.

"You think too much," she muttered to her reflection in the glass, dropped a bill on the table and hurried outside.

It was full dark now, and most of the stores up Centre were closed. She watched as a policeman walked into the station house behind a young man whose head was bowed, a woman in a light cloth coat trailing and wringing her hands. An ambulance several blocks down darted across the avenue, siren stilled, lights blaring. There was no traffic as she crossed, walked north toward her car, only the faintly hazed neon of a few late-keeping shops, the muffled footfalls of a handful of pedestrians passing like autumnal ghosts beneath street lamps that had not been redesigned since they'd been fired with gas. Her car was the only one still parked on the street. The color seemed grey, and she postponed walking to it by standing in front of . . .

She grinned.

*Her* shop.

Virtually all her savings transformed into plate glass, into a threshold, into the darkness beyond where there were black-wire bookracks forming three aisles back to front, and ceiling-high wooden ones she'd stained herself. The door was recessed, and she imagined it blocked so incredibly soon with brown cartons and brown boxes steel-banded and wire-taped, from which she would snatch glimpses of other worlds, other people, and sell them as dreams. Sections for lovers, for planet-hoppers, for clue-hunters, for children; a nod to the classics, to the drama, to lines of poetic conscience. But mostly, she knew, there would be the dreams.

Yarrow's Burrow.

She grimaced and decided the name could wait.

Turned, stepped off the curb and stopped herself with a shudder, glancing fearfully to her right.

There was no limousine.

She raised the collar of her raincoat to her cheeks, held it and hurried across to the car as she fumbled with her free hand for the keys in her purse. Unlocked the door and settled behind the wheel.

Switched on the ignition. And sat there. Staring. Finally looking over to the place that was now her own and wondering if the Station was as bad as she thought. Or if it was only her—Cindy/Cyd/Cynthia—champing, snarling at the successes her brothers had had while she herself had not yet found the direction she wanted her own life to take. At twenty-seven she should have done, she kept telling herself; if not a career, then a family. But none of the professions she knew or studied interested her enough, and none of the men had been interesting either, to a degree that had made her want to learn if they were caring.

Poor little rich girl, Ed had said once when they'd argued over something she'd already forgotten. A cliché like most, not entirely without substance.

Spoiled, too, she decided, was a good enough word. Everything when she needed it, everything when she wanted.

"You know," she told the windshield that fogged at her words, "if you keep thinking like this, lady, you're going to have to find a decent cliff around here to practice your diving."

She grinned, almost laughed, and drove down to Chancellor where she turned right with a glance to the police station, and had nearly reached the Chancellor Inn when a movement above her made her look in the rearview mirror.

The limousine.

The steering wheel shook under her hands, and she wished for no reason that she'd worn her driving gloves.

Coincidence, she thought. The man's done his business in one place, probably over dinner with a banker or two, and is now on his way to somewhere else. There are lots of limousines in Oxrun, they're practically a dime a dozen. Coincidence. It would be irrational to believe anything else. And paranoid. Not, she told herself, to mention stupid.

She obeyed the stop sign at the avenue's end and looked out to Mainland Road and the deserted fields that stretched to the horizon on the opposite side. She remembered an orchard that had been there once, one she used to raid with friends until the grower had died and the trees had gone with him. A fire. She thought she recalled a fire had destroyed them; but now, with no moon, she could see nothing but black.

The windshield fogged again and she switched on the blower, lowered her window slightly and was ready to move onto the highway when the car jumped forward, the wheel twisting in her hands. She swore and looked over her shoulder. The limousine was directly behind her, its bumper and half the grille below her line of sight. It pushed at her again, and she shook a fist at it. "All right, all right," she muttered. "Idiot bigshots think they own the road." And before it could bump her a third time she accelerated and spun right, heading for the traffic light that marked Williamston Pike.

Looked in the mirror and saw the limousine following.

Rapidly. Closing.

Passing beneath one of the mercury arc lights, its grey now blending to cover its windows.

And its headlights were dark.

Instinctively, she pressed her foot down and the car responded in kind. It shuddered once, almost faltering, before barreling ahead, past the Pike, past the light, and into the hills.

The limousine followed.

She gripped the steering wheel at ten and two, tried for a deep breath and failed. Sat as straight as she could to keep tension from her spine and stared at the headlights boring through the black. She was glad she could not see the trees, knowing they would be little more than a blur to measure her speed. Her left foot tapped the worn carpeting impatiently, her left hand's fingers releasing and regripping the beveled wheel one at a time. A dust-devil of leaves swirled in front of the car and was flattened, another stayed on the shoulder to tell her of the wind. The car swayed to the left; she righted it with barely a touch, grinning until she looked up to the mirror and saw the Greybeast following.

Its lights were on now, their glare catching her gaze and almost blinding her.

Stupid, she thought. What the—

The car hissed around a sharp bend and, before she could fully understand what she was doing, she slammed on the brakes and fought the car's skid as she thumped onto the graveled shoulder and punched off the lights. She was facing slightly downhill, beyond the curve, and within moments the limousine flashed behind her, its headlights stabbing at the sky as though searching for bombers, dipped and swung past her. In absolute silence.

She wasted no time waiting for the driver to realize his error. Immediately the taillights were no more than a prick, she made a clumsy U-turn that scraped the right front fender against a telephone pole and raced back toward the village, not realizing her headlights were still out until an oncoming car screamed its horn at her and swerved sharply, as though she had crossed the center line.

At the Pike she turned left into the village and pulled over to the curb after taking the first corner. Her hands would not leave the wheel. Her foot would not leave its pressure on the brake. The green dashlight wavered, blurred, picked up the quivering of her lips and arms, merged with the dark when the tears finally came. Silently. Quickly. As quickly gone as they had come. She licked at her lips, tried to shake her head and discovered the aching that throbbed at her temples, swept along her jaw where she'd kept her teeth clenched. The taste of blood—her lip. The smell of the old and cracked vinyl upholstery, of gasoline, of wet tarmac, of what had to be fear. Slowly, one by one, she willed her fingers free of the wheel and flexed them to banish the cramps in the joints. Rubbed at her temples. Her chest.

"God!" she said finally, and almost wept again at the sound of her voice.

# THREE

There were dreams in soft shifting colors of Cindybright days and Cynthiagrown nights, of Windsor Castle and Stonehenge at winter's dawn, of parties that lasted until the moon grew weary; of late December evenings in the family library when the fire was companion and the books her only friends; of Paul and Iris Lennon and Wallace McLeod, and the rest of the Yarrow staff who faded one by one in spite of the wealth; of Ed and his laughter and the smooth ride of his patience. Of winter nights . . . of Ed . . . of Paul, Iris, Wallace . . . Ed . . . and his laughter . . . of Ed . . . and winter nights . . .

And there were nightmares in colors that dared have no name; of her mother lying helpless at the foot of a steel ladder, her back twisted and broken while her mouth opened in scolding for the hands reaching to help her; of a pair of bright lights that shattered the walls to bring down the ceiling; of a faceless man *stop* who drove a monstrous car that expanded to cover the highway in a blackred rush; of driving between two hills *stop* whose incredible trees uprooted themselves and created a wall that reached out with barked claws to strip away the sky and *stop!* the breath from her lungs; of running across the park from the playing fields to the pond and seeing behind her a vast *stop!* shadowed figure that plucked at the stars and punctured the moon and *stop stop* lay in her path the sightless bloody corpses of Wallace and Paul and Iris *Stop* and *Stop!* Ed *Stop!* Ed *please stop* Ed *please* . . .

"Stop," she whispered, almost whimpered, twisted herself violently onto her side and opened her eyes.

The horrifying image of the bodies lingered, finally faded as she willed it, and the room returned in soft stages of light.

Bookcases fronted in glittering leaded glass, a tall polished wardrobe—her grandmother's—with the right-hand door that seldom stayed closed, dresser, vanity table and worn velvet stool, an overstuffed armchair with oversized wings she'd used as a child to carry herself away. Gentle reds and bronzed golds that shimmered in the morning light easing through the window—a casement window whose myriad small panes on every chilled morning seemed less like glass than thin slivers of ice. A book lay on the floor, its marker beside it. A pewter tray with crystal decanter and matching glass on the nightstand beside the bed. Prints on the walls of Remington cowboys and Remington squaws.

All there, she thought as she rolled onto her back, and winced at the clammy sheets that pressed to her spine. Immediately she sat up, swung her legs over the side and stood, hugging her nightgown to her chest as she moved to the window and looked down at the yard. Warm; until she was reminded of the month; and cold as she rubbed her arms vigorously, stretched and rolled her neck to banish the night's stiffness.

Brother, she thought, I don't need dreams like that anymore.

By the time she had managed to find the courage to drive home, dinner had been over for nearly an hour. Barton was locked in the library with his sons, and her mother was drying what remained of the meal's dishes. There'd been voices in the living room from a television set that cast purple shadows from a show she didn't recognize; and she had wandered silently, wishing the house a cottage instead of a mansion, a place where there weren't quite so many caverns where a Greybeast could hide. And when, toward eleven, she'd told the family what had happened—forgetting in the telling all her planned dramatic gestures —they had listened politely, quietly, only her mother nodding thoughtfully to show she'd been listening. The others seemed more interested in the television screen.

And when she had done, they had waited. Without speaking.

"Well," she'd finally exploded in exasperation, "isn't anyone going to say anything?"

Rob adjusted his glasses carefully. Evan, who was lying on the floor with a book cradled between his forearms, only lifted his head long enough to show her a shrug.

"Good God, people, I could have been killed!"

"Nonsense," her mother said. "It was nothing more than joyriders, or whatever they call those idiots these days. A woman alone in a car, a dark night . . . someone from the college, most likely, that's all. Good grief, Cynthia, this is Oxrun Station, not someplace like Detroit. You weren't in any real danger at all."

"Mother," she began, was cut off by her father's look.

"You were drinking at the Cove," he reminded her. "And I suspect you hadn't eaten yet, either. Your sensations were heightened and some fool kid only aggravated them, like your mother said." He smiled, reached for her hand and patted it, twice. "Relax, my girl. Take it easy."

She had almost thought to argue further until she noticed the smirk on Rob's face and realized then how foolish she must have seemed.

Moreso now as she watched a series of high-columned clouds lumber across the startlingly blue sky. And below, on the lawn, a flock of agitated blackbirds scurrying over the grass in cockheaded search of an early meal. From where she stood, she could easily imagine herself coasting in a small plane, watching a herd of dark cattle grazing in a field. She grinned. Imagination. A useful commodity had she been a writer or a teacher or someone in research. But, as she felt a swelling of gas burn in her stomach, she knew that her father had been right in his explanation. No food, the drink, and nerves about the shop. Her tolerance for liquor was remarkably low, most especially wine. It generally did not take more than a glass or two to dull her, make her drowsy. And in a way, she considered it a blessing. She had never been able to take enough to get drunk; she always fell asleep first, to the dismay of her escorts.

Nevertheless, the experience had been frightening, and if she ever caught the driver who had played games with her nerves . . .

She shook her head vigorously and reached up to stretch, feeling the dried perspiration of her nightmares pulling at her skin. She grimaced her disgust and ran a hand lightly over her stomach as if her palm could sponge that away too. Then, after a final look at the trees and the yard—and a fleeting image of her shack —she hurried into the marbled bathroom and took a long, steaming shower. Dressed. Took the stairs down two at a time.

She was whistling when she reached the dining room, stopped when she saw her mother the only one there, lingering over a cup of coffee and a piece of burnt toast. She grinned. Ever since the staff had been dismissed—where had she been then? in Rome? in Venice?—Myrtle had tried to live up to the enviable reputation Iris Lennon had left behind her. She never quite made it, however, according to Cyd's brothers, and it had not been long before meals in the house became a haphazard matter, each of the children virtually scurrying to get their own food before their mother assaulted what remained of the larder.

She stood at the sideboard and from a pewter pot poured herself coffee, sat opposite her mother at the long walnut table and watched her. Blue eyes met blue, and the older woman smiled.

"Are you feeling better, dear?"

"Silly," she said, using the coffee's aroma to waken her first. She spooned in sugar, stirred idly, and waited.

"Well, I shouldn't feel too silly if I were you," her mother said with a brief wave of an unringed hand. "I remember when your father and I, we were about your age, I think, we were driving down to New York. In what poor Angus wants to believe were the good old days. Highways, of course, weren't the same then. They were a good deal smaller, and lots of nice scenery. They also acted like launching pads, of course they didn't have them in those days either, launching pads for a million trucks. Huge things, I remember. Moving so fast they were gone before you could blink.

"I remember . . . yes, if memory serves, it was snowing, not too badly, but snowing I think it was, and this idiot milk tanker thing, the ones that look like oil trucks, it rode our tail for at least five miles once we'd crossed the state line. Your father, of course, he wouldn't budge at all, wouldn't give the man an inch, not on his life. He wouldn't move over to let the man pass, and he wouldn't speed up to give us some distance in case he had to stop short. That," she said with a touch to the paisley kerchief that bound her hair tightly, "is when I started to go grey. I swear, Cynthia, he nudged us once, but don't tell your father I said that because he'll swear I was drunk at the time."

"Were you?" Her expression was pure innocence though her lips worked at a smile.

Myrtle laughed. "I don't know, to tell the turth, it was so long ago now. But, between you and me, I probably was."

"You don't drink much these days, though, do you?"

Myrtle looked at her sharply, dropped her gaze to her cup where she studied the swirls of light and dark. "When the occasion demands," she said after a moment. "Will you be hanging around the house tonight, dear?"

Cyd remembered the party and stifled a premonition. "Oh, I don't know. Probably not. There's a film over in Harley I'd like to see. James Bond takes on the world again. I don't know. Why?" As if, she thought, I didn't know.

Myrtle shrugged a poor indifference. "Well, it should be rather interesting here for a change, dear. I'd . . . well, frankly, I'd like you to stick around for a while, if you don't mind, of course. If you would. I really . . . I would like very much for you to meet Doctor Kraylin. Your moods these days—"

"There is nothing wrong with any of my moods," Cyd said, more sharply than she'd wanted. "It's this ridiculous changeable weather. And the holidays. You know that, Mother. Thanksgiving, Christmas; times of joy and sadness, as some poet once said on the back of a greeting card. I've only been back a couple of months. I'm still getting reoriented. This is hardly Oxford Circus, you know. The sun's out now, though. I feel much better, really I do."

"Well, I want you to meet him anyway. I think you'll like him. He's . . . different."

Cyd watched her mother's eyes for a moment, not entirely sure she'd heard the tone she thought. Then she lowered her head and looked up at her. "Mother," she said in good-natured warning, "are you trying to do what I think you're trying to do?"

Myrtle instantly raised her hands, palms out, and shook her head. "Me? I'm your mother, Cynthia. What you do with your life is your own business. That has always been my credo—"

"Credo?"

"—and I try to live by it."

"Sure, Mother. Do what I want, as long as I'm married while I get about it."

"Now, Cynthia, I didn't say that."

Cyd kept her comments to herself while Myrtle reached for a pitcher of water and poured herself a glass. Water slopped over the rim, staining the linen place mat, and she clucked as she pushed the glass to one side, knocked it with her elbow and sent it shattering to the floor. Cyd rose, sat again when hissed at, heard a muttered curse when Myrtle reached over to pick up the pieces.

"You all right? You want—"

Myrtle sat up again, sucking at one finger. "No problem, dear. Caught a piece in my hand, that's all. I'll live. I won't bleed to death, if that's what you're worried about." She took a handkerchief from her hip pocket and wrapped it tightly around the wound, grinning and wincing alternately until the bandaging was done.

"Mother," she said, pointing at the cloth, "that's an expensive—"

"Big deal, so it stains. I've got hundreds, you know."

"Sure." She watched the finger morbidly, almost hoping for blood, then gave it up and emptied her cup. "All right, then. I think I'm off."

"What about tonight?"

"Mother, you're impossible, and I love you, too." She rose, rounded the table and kissed the woman solidly on top of her head. "You win, though. I'll stick around to meet this guy, if you really want me to."

"He's a doctor."

"Good for him. Maybe he can have a look at your back."

"There's nothing wrong with my back, young lady."

"Sure, Mother, whatever you say."

The silence could have been awkward, but Cyd moved on quickly, not stopping until she reached the hall. "By the way, I think I'll be dropping in on Iris and Paul this afternoon, if anyone wants me."

Myrtle set her cup carefully on its saucer, so slowly Cyd had to blink to be sure that it had moved. "Now why would you want to do a thing like that?"

"Why not?" she said, pushing her hair back from her forehead. "Actually, I had a dream about them last night, and I haven't gone to see them since I've been back, so . . ." and she shrugged.

"What about your shop? Shouldn't you be doing something there?" When her daughter stared, Myrtle only allowed a slow, unrepentant smile. "Your father never keeps secrets well, dear. When he came back grousing about Angus, I gave him a brandy, sat in his lap, and . . ."

"Well?"

"Well what? You want my approval? All right, you have it. You want me to argue, you're crazy. I'm too old to argue with you, and besides, you're not stuffy enough to do what your brothers do."

"Mother!"

"They may be my children, dear, but I know they're stuffy."

Cyd left behind a cloud of laughter, not realizing until she noted the empty stalls in the garage that she hadn't seen her brothers at all since last night. Saturdays aren't sacred anymore, she thought sadly as she drove off the estate; used to be you could sleep until noon and not care who knew it. Times change, old girl, times change.

But not the Lennons.

They had come in from Hartford when she was ten, stayed on until only a few months before she'd finished her tour. Iris: tall, thin, so inordinately fleshless she barely cast a shadow, so deft in the kitchen she'd had dozens of offers from cosmopolitan restaurants to desert service and come into her own; she was also laconic to the point of spawning a rumor she was, in fact, mute. And Paul, her husband; as tall, as lean, somewhat confused by the times he lived through, and as garrulous as his wife was silent when the need arose and the gossip was fruitful. In all the years Cyd had known them—and from what she'd learned of their previous life—they had never been separated, not even for a night. And, curiously, Iris never cooked for herself at all. Once the Yarrows' meals were done, Paul took over, often panting in from the gardens just in time to duck Iris' glare.

Cyd had never known who among the children had been the Lennons' favorite, though there had to have been one. She always suspected it had to have been Rob, if only because of his

own taciturn temper, so much like Paul's when the old man was
alone.

Ten minutes later she turned off Chancellor Avenue onto
Hartwell Place, a one-block street, the last in the Station before
the three-mile stretch to the railroad depot. The houses here
were quiet, were old, were more shades of white and grey with
black trim than she'd thought was possible in such a short space.
There were no children here, nor pets of any note. It was, instead, a place of great spreading trees, of fragmented shade, of
rose bushes and lawns and lemonade on the porch.

The Lennons' home was in the block's center, and she pulled
into the graveled drive with more than a touch of nerves and anticipation. The house was a single-story, with a peeling plaster
fawn beside the front stoop, and a series of thick hanging plants
now browned by the weather, hung from the clapboard from the
door to the screened porch that bordered the drive. She sat,
watched, saw no signs of living and wondered suddenly if perhaps she shouldn't have called them first.

Iris would be reserved no matter what happened; but Paul
needed time to gather himself—his clothes and his mind never
could take surprises.

A curtain fluttered in the house next door, and Cyd grinned as
she slid from the car and moved to the front door. There was
the unmistakable aroma, then, of baked bread and homemade
soups, biscuits and cookies she knew were only memories, but
she was glad that the memories at least still had not changed.

She rang the bell, waited, was about to ring a second time
when she heard someone calling from around the back. She hesitated, then moved quickly to the drive, trying to walk as quietly
as possible along the gentle curve that swung to a garage at the
house's far side. The lawn was vaguely unkempt, and at the edge
of the grass were two wicker chairs; and in them the Lennons,
bundled to the neck, each wearing a woolen cap pulled down to
their ears.

She stopped and smiled, hands clasped in front.

They watched her for several long seconds before Paul suddenly launched himself from his chair, pale lips grinning as his
hands took hers and held them.

"Be darned, Iris," he said without turning around. "Be darned
and damnation, it's Miss Cindy back to us for a chat."

Iris, unchanged, only nodded. Once in recognition. She wore thick-lensed glasses that reflected the house, hiding her eyes though her mouth finally curled into a welcoming smile as her husband led Cyd to his chair and bade her sit. Then he stood facing the both of them, hands tight behind his back.

"My Lord," he said, looking quickly from the girl to his wife. "My Lord, it's been . . . well, it's been over a year, hasn't it, dear?"

Iris nodded.

Like a movie set, Cyd thought as she examined the paint peeling from the house, the uncut browning grass, the clutter by the garage. The front is one thing, the back another.

"What do you say, Missy?"

She broadened the smile that was splitting her cheeks. "I'm sorry, Paul, I was thinking. What did you say?"

"He said," Iris whispered, "would you like something to drink?"

"No. No, but thanks." She gestured at the chairs, then, and the weak setting sun. "Isn't it awfully cold to be sitting out here like this? I'd think you'd catch your death."

Paul, his neck wrapped in a crimson muffler that matched to a shade his quilted hunting jacket, chuckled and shook his head. "Sun's the best for you, Missy, even this time of year. We try to get at least an hour a day. Vitamin C, you understand." He paused as if waiting for Iris to comment, then squatted easily to his haunches and made a fist of both hands. "Well, what brings you here, Missy? You don't mind if we still call you Missy, do you? A lot of years' habit that one is. You certainly have better things to do than see old fogies like us."

"Ain't old," Iris said.

"True enough," he said quickly.

They waited.

While she tried to inspect them without seeming rude. At least in their middle-seventies they were but apparently still well in control. Paul's hawked nose was slightly red, Iris' stub peeling dry skin: no purple beneath the eyes, the chins if anything even more pointed, and not even Paul could hide the taut wattles. The crusty New England stereotype, she thought; and if people didn't know their names, didn't know them by sight, then seeing them together would give them pause—from one to the other their sex was hidden.

The distant cry of the afternoon train fit snugly into the November silence, and it was several minutes more before Cyd suddenly began to talk without introduction: about the store, her sometimes ludicrous struggles to come up with a name, the afternoons she'd spent in the toy store with Dale Blake learning what it took to run a small business. "Of course," she added, "there are special things that come with just the books. I sent for I don't know how many pamphlets and things from the Small Business people, and went to a couple of government seminars over in Hartford just before I left the country. I don't know if I can do it, or at least do it right, but I do know one thing—I'm going to need some help."

"College kids," Iris suggested tersely. "They're always looking for things to do. Come around here twice, three times a week wanting the odd job, things like that. Paul sends them away. I don't trust them."

"Right," Paul said with a nod for emphasis.

Another short pause while Cyd waited for her courage. Then, "Do you two like it here? Really like it, I mean?" and knew her hunch had been right when she saw the look that passed between them. The Lennons had worked for too many years, were too wrapped in the Protestant Ethic to enjoy their new life. They were bored, and from the looks of the house and grounds, they didn't have enough money to do anything about it.

"All right, then," she said, smiling and leaning forward with her arms on her knees. "I want to try to open a week from Monday, to catch the tail end of the Christmas season if I can. I'm going to need your help, Paul, Iris. I'd like . . . well, I'd really be pleased if you two could come and work with me."

"Hate charity," Paul said immediately, rising to stand behind his wife.

"It isn't charity, and you know it," she said sternly, more to Iris than to him. "I talked with Bella Innes, you know—she works with Dale in the toy store?—and she told me how you two have been dropping in on Mr. Carlegger now and then."

"Fat old busybody," Paul said angrily.

"Oh, hush up," Iris told him, and pulled off her glasses. Her eyes, watery and pale, searched for Cyd, found her and held. "Your father has been very kind to us, Missy. He didn't have to give us a pension, but he did. 'Course, now that he has a little trouble he can't always pay. Now, Mr. Carlegger, he runs a pretty good place for getting folks jobs, we know that. Trouble is, we're of an age, you know, and—" She looked helplessly toward the house, and Cyd rose at once, clapping her hands.

"It's settled, then. My first shipment should be coming in on Wednesday. Shall I see you at the shop, say, ten o'clock?"

"So late?" Paul said, his grin grotesquely wide.

"Plenty early enough until I get used to it, you miserable slavedriver," she said. Impulsively, then, she kissed Iris' cheek and shook Paul's hand firmly. The silence that followed was tinged with grateful embarrassment, and she hurried away before the moment was spoiled. As an afterthought, she turned at the corner of the porch and called back to Paul, "I was thinking about talking to Wallace, too. Does he still live off King Street, down by the hospital?"

Her smile, already growing in anticipation of theirs, froze when Paul dropped abruptly into his chair and shook his head slowly. Iris reached over to pat at his arm, pushed herself awkwardly to her feet and walked with a slight sideways limp up the drive. A hard look, and she took Cyd's arm to lead her to the front.

"Iris," she said, her voice low to a whisper, "what is it? Did I say something wrong?"

"Hush, child, you didn't say anything." She stopped when she saw the blue automobile, clucked loudly and passed a hand over her chin. "Lord, ain't you got rid of that thing yet? Should have had it condemned ten years ago." She did not wait for a response, only opened the door and eased Cyd in, closed it and leaned over when the window was rolled down. "Wallace's dead, child. I thought you . . . I would have thought your father told you about it."

"No. God, no, Iris, I didn't know." She fumbled for a word. "They never said a word. I . . . how?"

The old woman tapped a large-knuckled finger on the steering wheel. "We don't know for sure. Doctor claims it was his heart. He was walking back from his day in the park last . . . oh, last

August, I think it was. You was still away, anyway. He came up to the police station and just keeled over. Just like that. There wasn't anything anyone could do for him. Doctor claims he was dead before he hit the sidewalk, he says."

"Come on, Iris," she said. "His heart? Good Lord, Wallace could lift—"

"I know, I know," Iris said. "But that's the way of it sometimes, I suppose. You go all your natural life, not a sick day to your name, and when your time comes whether you're ready or not—" and she snapped her fingers, looked back toward the yard. "Paul, he took it hard. Still does, in fact. He keeps checking his pulse, things like that. They was the same age, you know. Seventy-two almost to the day." She straightened suddenly. "It happens," she said. "Now get off. We'll be there, don't you worry. We ain't never let you down yet, not for twenty years. And Missy . . . Miss Yarrow . . ."

Cyd could not meet the expression that worked the old woman's face. Instead, she switched on the ignition and raced the engine once. "Wednesday," she said after a cough at her lap. "And Iris, thanks, really. To tell you the truth, I don't trust those college kids, either."

There was a brief moment when she thought Iris Lennon would release a rare laugh. But it passed, and the best the woman had was another slight curling of those thin, bloodless lips. Cyd waved then, and backed into the street.

Poor Wallace, she thought as she turned the car around.

But as she reached the corner and looked up into the mirror, she wondered for a second who was the worse off—the Lennons or Wallace McLeod.

Iris was still on the front lawn, bending over stiffly to pick up a dead branch. When she straightened, she stared at the car, tossed the branch into the gutter and vanished around the side of the house.

When she was gone the street was lifeless again, and Cyd could not repress a shudder as she made the left turn and headed back for the village center.

Who was worse off? she wondered again, and did not like the answer that came immediately to mind.

# FOUR

"I was hoping you'd be the first, you and that dumb, beautiful white plume."

She had been leaning against the hood of the car and staring at the shop when Bella Innes, Dale Blake's assistant at the toy store, had hurried over to tell her she'd accepted a delivery. The cartons were in Bartlett's storeroom. Cyd had been unable to breathe. She hadn't expected anything to come until Monday at the earliest.

Now, suddenly, it had begun.

When she wasn't looking, her first dreams had arrived.

Twenty minutes later she was alone in a skeletonwork forest of racks and shelves and banded brown boxes. Her hands trembled. Her eyes watered. And she'd thought it an augury more favorable than a vaulted soaring eagle that the first carton she'd opened carried on top a half-dozen copies of her childhood lover. Setting aside the invoice sheet, she'd picked out the paperbound book and carried it reverently to that section she had marked with a hand-lettered sign laboriously fashioned for the marking of the Drama.

In the center at the top.

The tears were unashamed that soaked her cheeks, were absorbed into her sweater as she set Cyrano in his place. Then she stepped back to examine the Gascon's profile, the sweep of his burgundy hat, the cloud of his plume. She began to laugh without the tears stopping, felt her legs grow weak and she sat on the floor.

With a single slash of his rapier, deBergerac had broken the spell; the waiting was done.

The papers and Angus Stone had been one thing, the laying out of cash and the purchase of the books, the shelves, the decorations in comforting gay colors; but this was different. This was the multifold calling of her account, and the danger of her not answering was distressingly evident: her name, for one—why should people patronize someone who didn't need money? her experience for another—how many invoices and bills and charges would she bungle, and what would the errors mean to her success? and her own strength—even in failure if failure there was, would she be able to stay away from her father, her brothers, would she be able to fall on her own without grasping for the support she knew would be there, just waiting for the asking? There was no question she had to do it, no question she must at all costs consider herself in effect disowned by her family.

She was on her own.

She had to be, or none of it now would have been worth the anguish.

The afternoon dwindled.

The counter she placed jutting out from the doorjamb, and on it a small-shaded lamp she'd used when she'd come after everyone had gone to bed. During those late nights she had stained the wallshelves and painted the walls, lay carpeting on the floor, lettered section signs, sketched through a ream of oversized paper the displays she had wanted to mark the seasons and the best sellers and the impulses to feature those books she loved that ordinarily might vanish without a trace of a read.

The afternoon faded.

The floor was littered with empty cartons and crumpled papers. Invoices were stacked haphazardly on the counter. And while she worked still another delivery came. She did not care. She wiped the perspiration from her brow and dragged the books in, stacked them and filed them and every few minutes sat down to read. She'd long since stopped laughing, long since stopped crying, and her smile became fixed, her cheeks aching delightfully with what was no effort at all. And it wasn't until she'd counted and set the last copies of the last box that she realized the time.

Lord, she thought, Mother's going to have a fit.

But she could not leave. Not yet. Not now. There was an irrational apprehension growing with the shadows—that if she left now the store and the books and the shelves would disappear;

that when she returned Monday morning there would be a sunless gap between Bartlett's and the Station Savings and Loan. An alley that led nowhere because whatever had been there had not existed at all.

It took her over an hour to find the courage to lock the door, another ten minutes before she relaxed and grinned. The sun was gone, and she pulled her short coat closed to her throat, walked up to the luncheonette where she ate a large salad while she worried at the logistics of the Lennons coming to work. She was glad Iris and Paul would be with her at the start; it was their support she needed more than their hands. Iris' quick nods and Paul's infectious smile. Even if they put up with her for only a week, it would be enough. After that . . . well, there was always, she thought, those damned college kids.

And it wasn't until she'd locked the car up for the night and was staring at the drive lined with her parents' guests' elegance that she looked down at herself and remembered her appearance. Dust and ink smudged over her face, her sweater, the faded baggy jeans. Her loafers so scuffed the original color could have been anything at all from oxblood to brown. She considered sneaking in through the kitchen, but dismissed it at once— her grandfather had for some reason closed off the back stairs, so she would have to move into the foyer anyway. Move in, and be seen. But as long as Barton didn't see her, she guessed it would be all right.

"For crying out loud," she whispered harshly to herself then as she opened the front door. "Cindy, you're not sixteen."

She could not help it; she stopped in the middle of the hall and stared. In the sitting room were close to three dozen people, all of them her parents' age or older, all of them dressed almost as casually as she. Slowly she crossed to the threshold and leaned against the jamb, arms folded loosely over her chest. Three dozen and quiet, drifting in and out of the dining room, standing in front of the fireplaces and watching the low dancing flames. She could see the end of a buffet in the dining room, and several of the guests were scattered over the divans and chairs, paper plates on their knees, their thighs, smiling and chatting softly with their neighbors.

Simple fare, she noted with a quick puzzled frown.

From speakers hidden in the walls drifted muted strains of semi-classical melodies too soft to really listen to, yet loud enough to obscure the fact that virtually no one at the party was talking above a whisper.

She could not believe it. While there was laughter, it was gentle; while there was movement, it was ghosting. She listened for but did not hear her mother's braying laugh, nor her father rising Olympian in defending a political position. Yet these two things were if nothing else staples for the house parties she attended or avoided; they were expected, and they were missing. And for a moment she wondered if her parents were even there.

"Cynthia! Darling!"

She sighed. So much for Mother.

She pushed away from the frame and watched as Myrtle—in an embroidered peasant blouse down from her sharp-edged shoulders, and snug, black velvet toreador pants—moved in her direction, holding the hand of a man she dragged behind her. He was short, slender, dressed in white turtleneck and blue blazer, black trousers and white shoes. His hair was dark and brushed straight back from his forehead, his face heavily lined though it seemed more a case of natural direction than lashes of age. Not at all bad looking, she thought as she prepared a greeting smile; if he'd shave off that stupid beard, or at least grow a mustache to go with it, he might even be handsome.

"Cynthia, where have you been?" The scold was meaningless, but not the look that examined her clothing, the smears on her hands and face, the disarrangement of her hair. "Have you been toiling in the mines, dear?"

Cyd swallowed a tart comment in deference to the man. "A shipment came in unexpectedly at the store, Mother, and I lost track of the time. But we needn't talk about that now, need we?"

Myrtle accepted the statement-more-than-a-question by immediately stepping to one side and, with a regal detachment that nearly caused her daughter to break into laughter, introduced her to Doctor Calvin Kraylin, director and chief financial underwriter for the Station's Kraylin Clinic.

"I'm afraid I don't know where that is," she said, taking back her hand quickly, trying not to be obvious in wiping it on her hip. "Not in town, surely."

"Of course not," he said politely, his voice unnaturally high. "It's about three miles from here, out on the Pike. You may have seen the entrance if you've ever had occasion to ride into the valley."

"There are nothing but farms and unused fields out there, Doctor. I seldom go that way."

He smiled briefly, folding his hands into his pockets. "Lovely home you have here, Miss Yarrow."

"Well," Myrtle said, already moving, "I'll leave you two to get better acquainted. Have a good time, Cal. And Cynthia, please comb your hair, dear. My friend will think I'm not a good mother."

Kraylin bowed; Cyd smiled. A few words then about nothing she could remember, then or afterward. The awkwardness of two people thrown into company for no good reason and against each other's will, each instinctively on guard against the other. It was as though, Cyd thought, they were competing for territory, and immediately told herself the reaction was foolish. Yet she could not quite shake the unmistakable impression that the doctor would have rather been with those twice his age than with her. She nearly made a move to free him, but when he requested almost shyly a visitor's tour of the house, she agreed readily— eager to be able to talk and keep her nervousness, and her anger, at bay for the time being.

It was as bad as she thought it would be.

He was properly appreciative of the oils done of her family, of the woodwork, the furniture, the carpeting, the paint; he exclaimed wonderment at the insertion of the television and the stereo equipment into the two fireplaces in the living room and remarked aloud at the curiously fitting juxtaposition; he nodded at the silverware, the sideboards, the wainscoting; and sidestepped politely her questions about the clinic and its functions, giving her the impression he used it primarily for those wealthy hypochondriacs whose family physicians had thrown up their hands. Yet he had saved the family, she reminded herself sternly, so he couldn't be a quack no matter how he chose to run his practice.

Judge not, she thought, and knew it was impossible.

By the time they returned to the sitting room they were silent, and had been for five minutes. Cyd was feeling more and more gritty and wanted a hot shower; the doctor kept licking his full lower lip and stroking the beard too perfectly trimmed to seem anything but staged.

Myrtle was waiting. She grabbed both Kraylin's hands, pumped them once and waved him past and into the nearest knot of people who were obviously expecting him.

"Well," she said then, plucking a cigarette from a leather case and lighting it with gold. "Well, what do you think?"

Cyd took her time, until the doctor and his coterie had moved out of range. "He's a creep."

The smoke from her mother's nostrils was a dragon's fair warning. "Marvelous," she said. "One of the best minds in the Station, if not the state, and you say he's a creep. Cynthia, when are you going to grow up?"

Cyd raised her eyebrows in exasperation. "Mother, he may be all that you say, and probably is," she added quickly to forestall an interruption, "but that doesn't mean he has to be a saint in his personal life."

"Are you saying he made a pass at you back there?"

"No, Mother, but he certainly doesn't fit the picture he wants to give, does he? Dashing yachtsman, artistic beard and sweep of the hair . . . with a voice like somebody's got a hand around his throat. And about as scintillating a conversationalist as a million-year rock."

Someone dropped a glass; there was a flurry of napkins.

The music came on louder, and a woman in a bandana raised her voice in complaint.

Myrtle blew a smoke ring, watched it, blew another. "He saved our lives, you know."

Not willing to accept the sudden thrust of guilt, Cyd clicked refusal with her tongue and turned to face the foyer. "You could have gone to the hospital, you know."

"Cynthia, you know better than that."

"All right, Mother, all right, so he saved your lives." She

frowned and turned back, snatched an invisible thread from the older woman's shoulders. "I don't get it. What do you want from me, an approval or something?" She grinned. "Seems to me I've already heard that once today, haven't I? Well, okay, you've got it, are you satisfied? He's a good doctor, I'll take your word for it. But does that mean I have to trust him with my life, too?"

"Suppose you get sick?"

She lay a gentle hand on her mother's bare shoulder, wishing at the same time she could tell her how ridiculous she looked. "There is, if you recall, someone named Foster. He's a doctor, as I recall. And as I recall further, he dragged me bloody into his bloody world with a flat pair of forceps without my permission."

"You don't have to be sarcastic, Cynthia."

She sighed, loudly. "You're right, Mother, and I'm sorry. I must be—" She scanned the room once more, saw there was little more animation than when she had left, though the volume was growing louder and the company more relaxed. "Look, I've had an unexpectedly hard day, and I'm tired and need some rest."

Myrtle's scowl dissolved instantly into an attitude of apology. "And I'm sorry, too, dear. I should have noticed. Why don't you get into the shower, wash off and, if you feel like it, come back down and join us."

Cyd shook her head. "Mother, please don't take offense, but there doesn't seem like much action going down here tonight. In fact, now that I mention it, I don't even think I know half these people."

"Friends come and go, dear. You've been away, remember?"

She refused to make comment, only kissed the woman's cheek and retreated to her rooms. As she undressed, slowly, listening to the shower thunder in her bathroom, she tried to guess what phase her parents were going through this time. It seemed to her that every half-decade or so they cleaned house of their friendships, like a literally personal spring cleaning. Of course there were always the stalwarts—Doc Foster, Angus Stone, a handful of others—but the fringe group was transient, almost mercurially so. One year it had been spiritualism, another year UFOs. She recalled a time when ecology was so important to her mother that she had been driven to give away every natural fur she owned, only to replace them with synthetics that were virtually as expensive as the ones she had sacrificed. There were the manias with history, with ESP, with . . . she grinned. She'd stopped keeping track after the last group made her dizzy.

She washed, dried, slipped into a plaid shirt and pressed jeans, decided that nothing was going to make her revisit a party that was more like a wake.

She tried some reading, but could not get past the third page of four novels.

She thought about going for a late night walk, but a touch to the panes that were more ice than glass made her shiver and step back. November was too quickly giving way to winter; and while she enjoyed exploring the last-season woods, it was still too damp, too . . . dead to be comfortable.

She looked at herself in the vanity mirror and grinned: All dressed up and no place to go.

No place. To go.

A conversation with her father not three weeks before:

*"If you don't mind me saying so, young lady, I have noticed a curious lack of what used to be called in my day gentlemen callers around here since you got back. It's not like the way it was before you went away. A curious lack, if you don't mind me saying."*

*"I don't have any."*

*"Why not?"*

*"I don't interest them, I guess."*

*"Nonsense. I don't believe that for a minute. You're still young, you're lovely, you're certainly not stupid."*

*"Men don't like women with brains, Father. That's one of the curses of being a Yarrow. Brains. Supposedly that means we threaten you, don't we?"*

*"I'm serious, young lady. I don't like this social life of yours at all."*

*"I don't seem to have any, Father."*

*"That's exactly what I mean, Cynthia. Who are you saving yourself for anyway? Some white knight on his charger gallumphing down the Pike to sweep you off into some magical safe valley? Be reasonable, Cynthia. Let me die happy."*

"Great. The way I reckon it, then, that gives me at least thirty years to dig up a husband."

"You're very disconcerting, you know, Cynthia."

"It runs in the family, Father."

"Cynthia—"

"Look, Father . . . look, as long as I can remember we've always worked under the agreement that my private life was exactly that—private. If and when I decide to step out again, to become the scourge of Oxrun Station and ruin hundreds of young men's lives, you'll be the first to know, believe me. But right now, I'm . . . not ready. I've too much to think about, and I'm not ready to go hunting for whatever you call it when men go hunting for quail."

"I don't like it."

"For crying out loud, Father, just leave me alone."

"Cynthia, you do not understand how important—"

"Father, I really don't want to fight with you."

"Now you listen to me, young woman, if it's that Grange fellow—"

She blinked and turned away from the mirror, suddenly realizing what it was she had been missing outside. All those automobiles—none less than five figures when it came to the buying —and there hadn't been a sign of a security guard from Ed's agency. Usually, one man in imposing uniform stood on the front stoop in plain view, a none-too-subtle warning that the patrols were out, more a psychological deterrent than anything else; at the same time, another man or two prowled the grounds without a flashlight and in civilian dark dress. At any party she had been to, either here or elsewhere, all the guards could be sensed if not seen; but tonight there was nothing. The grounds had been deserted.

Deciding to take a look around for herself—and admitting another minute alone in her rooms would drive her crazy—she grabbed a heavy, thigh-length navy cardigan from the wardrobe and made her way toward the steps. All the lights were out, visibility confined to the soft glow upward from the central shaft of the staircase. When she reached the railing that surrounded the core she stopped and frowned. At the front of the house was the distinct clear glow of a lamp through an open door, around the corner on the right. The nursery or her mother's rooms. She almost ignored it, had one foot on the top step before she caught herself again, her left hand kneading the waxed slope of the bannister. The light bothered her, but she was hesitant to investigate. From the moment she had been given her own rooms they had become, like all the others, inviolate; and even now, nearly three decades later, it always took an effort of will to enter someone else's suite without an invitation.

"It isn't going to bite," she muttered. "She'll have a fit if you don't turn it off."

Quickly, she moved around the stairwell and down the hall, made the corner with one hand trailing along the wall and stopped at the threshold to her mother's parlor. There was a rolltop desk set between the two outer windows and on it a package that caught the light and held it. Silver paper, bowed, the Bradford's Jeweler's insignia embossed clearly on the side. A summoned image of her mother in that ludicrous get-up, and she realized there wasn't a sparkle of gems on her; not around her neck, on her fingers, nothing on either wrist. Now why, she wondered, would she go to all that fuss about a new bracelet and then not even wear it? It wasn't like her not to show off a new acquisition to her friends. But then, she thought as she switched off the light, there was a lot about her family these days that wasn't really like them. A current of nervous energy that seemed to have no focus.

She shrugged and continued downstairs, was crossing the open foyer when she looked left and paused. The front room was empty, voices drifting in from the buffet though the connecting doors were now closed. A single laugh, multiplied, filling the spaces so silent before.

Cyd shook her head, thinking that the complaint parents never understand their children was an easily reversible oversimplification. One of these days, she thought with a grin when the laugh came again, I'm going to have to have a talk with them. They're getting too rowdy in their declining years.

# FIVE

Her hands nestled deeply in the sweater's pockets as she stood beneath the faintly bronze glow of the outside light, staring at the row of automobiles in the drive. They flared brief explosions of silver at her, of amber, of red, seemed all to be black though she knew there were midnights of blue and green, and one deep copper at the head of the line. There were no chauffeurs waiting, no high school attendants hired for the occasion. And she recalled a number of muggy summers too many years ago when lank men in tight uniforms lounged about the hoods, smoking, talking quietly, every so often carelessly wiping a chamois rag over a spot on a fender. Glamorous then, she wondered now what a life like that could possibly be. What did they think of, dream of, talk about, scheme? What was on their minds as they drove?

She took the few steps down in a single exuberant leap and walked to the nearest sedan, peered in at the glittering console and decided a jet pilot in his prime couldn't have more controls to worry at and play with. Her car was different; she drove it rather than steered it, something the owners of these cars couldn't possibly understand.

A husky whisper of wind brushed at the few leaves remaining on the trees and she straightened, sensing rather than seeing her breath fog from her lips. She began to walk, coming down hard on her low heels to listen to the sound, to banish the silence. The cold drew at her cheeks and tightened the skin, chapping her lips as she licked at them frequently to keep them moist. Something small scurried through the shrubs that hugged the house's base; she stared into the darkness, saw nothing and shrugged. Squirrel. Chipmunk. Nothing to do from season to season but protect a family and gather food against the snows.

When the drive began to curve inward toward the lane and the Pike, she left the concrete and walked over the grass. Frost had already begun to stiffen the blades, and she snapped them underfoot as though walking on cellophane. She scarcely ever paid much attention to this section of the grounds; they were and always had been solely for show. As children, she and her brothers had not been permitted to play here, and over the years they had lost whatever interest they might have had in displays of defiance. A new land, it seemed then, of alien slopes and dark pools that should have been water and were only odd shadows. Even the trees that masked the house from the road were different—blue-tinted spruce with broad heavy boughs in staggered rows that, when the wind blew, dragged on the brown-needled dirt. She wandered aimlessly toward them, breaking into a tuneless, comforting whistle as the cold slithered down the back of her neck.

There was no moon. There were no stars.

And the front door's light seemed weak as an ember.

She tripped on a rough-edged rock buried in leaves, stumbled sideways and felt a sharp twinge at her ankle. A testing, a wince, and she moved on again, paralleling the trees now as she headed back for the drive. Had someone been watching and she knew they'd been there, she would have manufactured a limp after her minor, careless spill; not a heavy one, but enough to show that she had sustained an injury and was carrying on in the best Yarrow tradition. Courage, she thought; that's what her father had demanded from them all. In finance, in school—the courage to take blows and not be stopped by them.

And part of her reason for fleeing to Europe . . . she grinned her melancholy at this first admission of the flight. Flight, not a trip. Flight from that selfsame courage that kept upper lips stiff as Grandfather's fortune was eaten by taxes, by larger competitors, by extravagance and waste. She had demanded her father do something about it, and in the library that night had seen him appear helpless. For the first time . . . helpless.

She had thought to make him angry enough to regain the advantage, to fight back with his sons the best way he could. But Evan had fallen into the same well of despair; only Rob had understood what she was trying to do, had tried to rally with her.

Had tried, and had failed. He was the middle child, though he often seemed the eldest, and she often wondered where the depths of his frustration ended. It was he, she had come to learn, who had instigated the firing of the Lennons and McLeod, had cut down on the parties, on the cars, on the grounds. An acre here, an acre there, until only five out of fifty were left to be tended. By Mother, when she felt like it; by a gardener when they could.

She found herself suddenly at the edge of the drive, one foot on the blacktop, the other balanced on the row of canted, white-washed bricks that set the circumference of the circle.

If it were true that things were so tight, she wondered if that was the reason for the vanishing gems. Was it possible—

"Is this a private meditation, or can anyone join in?"

With one hand to her chest she swallowed to set her heart back in its place, was momentarily proud of the way she had not leapt screaming for the nearest tall tree.

"I kind of thought you were out here," she said when her voice would work without trembling.

"You came looking?"

"Just checking," she said quickly, looking up as Ed moved to her side. "I wanted to see how the peasants had adapted to the Station's brand of cold."

He held out his hands, buried in thick gloves, and wrapped his arms over a dark woolen jacket to mime the blizzard he felt on the rising wind. He wore no hat; she had never seen him wear one. When he exaggerated a sneeze then, she patted his arm lightly in a show of patronizing sympathy before looking around at the shadows, at the shrubs and the trees.

"You alone?"

"Absolutely. It was a last-minute call from your father. I had a feeling it was only because he felt guilty."

"Well, you certainly don't have to worry about thieves to-night," she said with a pointed glance to the house. "What's in there now wouldn't tempt the devil. Strangest party I ever saw."

"You couldn't tell by me. I'm only here to see that these behe-moths don't get slaughtered at the curb."

A pause that became a silence. The distant growling thunder

of a truck on the Pike. The scurrying again that faded before the wind.

Ed suddenly snapped rigid, lay a hand on her shoulder and pulled her back off the drive. She frowned, followed his gaze and was about to question him when she saw, faintly, a dark figure moving along the outside of the line of cars from the far end. As it kept the vehicles between it and the house it bent down at each driver's door to peer inside while one hand tugged at the handle. Quickly, silently. With increasing agitation. By the time it had reached a point opposite the front door, she felt Ed readying to call out and she nudged him into silence. Then she stepped lightly over the brick row. The last car in line was the copper sedan. She leaned against the fender with her arms folded against her breast. Waiting. The figure too intent on the cars and the house to see her until it reached the rear bumper. Sensed her and looked up. The tempting option of flight was obvious in his attitude, disappointment flaring darkly over his face framed by a black and pulled down skull cap.

She tsked loudly. Twice.

He sagged and stood up, a full head taller than she.

"Looks like business is a little slow, huh, Sandy?" she said.

"Hi, Miss Yarrow. I guess you caught me, right?"

"Yeah, I guess I did."

Ed moved to stand behind her, but the boy's eyes did not leave her face.

"You guys going to call the police or something?"

"Why?" she said. "You haven't done anything yet."

The boy scratched at the side of his nose. "Intent, isn't that what they call it, Mr. Grange?"

"That's what they call it, son," Ed said. "You mind letting us in on the secret?"

From cap to shoes Sandy was dressed in flat black, and the pale cast of his face was harsh in contrast. He coughed into a fist. And the nervousness he'd been trying to control finally broke through and his hands flapped uselessly at his sides before diving into his pockets. A boot scuffed at the ground. He looked up without raising his head.

"I wasn't going to steal one. Not for good, anyway."

"I know that," Cyd said.

"I just wanted to leave it out on the Pike somewheres. Make them think it was gone, at least for a while."

Ed's voice was carefully neutral. "That would have been a lot of trouble for the Yarrows, you know, son. It would have been awfully embarrassing for them, what with the police coming around and their friends probably getting angry."

"But that's the point, isn't it?" said Cyd. "Well, I don't know about you two, but I'm freezing out here. Let's go inside. As long as we're going to have confessions and police brutality, we might as well be warm in the process."

"What? Miss Yarrow—"

She grinned. "Sandy, your grandfather and I were pretty close in what we folks call the old days. And Mr. Grange here knows you just about as well as I do, right? So let's go inside, the back way, and get something from the kitchen. I promise you now it's nothing my mother has cooked."

She refused to allow the boy any time to think. She took hold of his arm and led him quickly around the side of the house, knowing that Ed would follow dutifully—if only to find out what Wallace McLeod's grandson was doing back beyond the park. And by the time the pan had warmed the milk, the cocoa spooned out and dissolved while the three of them were seated around a huge oaken table, the boy's face had flushed and his eyes were puffing red.

"Come on, Sandy," she said gently. "Your folks didn't raise you to be a car thief. Give."

"It wasn't fair, Miss Yarrow," he said finally, staring through the steam that rose from his cup. "He was a good guy, my grandfather, and it wasn't fair that he was let go just like that." He snapped his fingers weakly, watched them retreat to hold the cup again. "I mean, he could work as good as me, you know what I mean? It killed him to have to leave this place, really it did. I mean, it killed him. He was too old to get another job, even though he was strong and all, and my mother said it was his heart that did it. It was broken."

"People don't break their hearts, not literally," she said softly, uncomfortable for the sensation of family guilt that had settled to her shoulders, weighting them, making them sag.

"I know that," he said angrily. "I know that, I'm not stupid.

But it killed him just the same. He shouldn't have died, Miss Yarrow. He was a strong man. His heart was just as good as yours or mine. But he . . . dropped. Just like that, he dropped."

"I know," she said, avoiding Ed's gaze. "As a matter of fact, I'm ashamed to say I only heard about it this afternoon. From Iris Lennon."

"Oh, that old bag."

"Sandy!"

The boy ducked his head quickly and muttered an apology without substance, sipped at his drink and grimaced when the burning chocolate scorched his tongue. He blew at the swirling surface before looking to Ed. "He was going to the police, you know."

"I knew he was in front of the station when it happened, yes," Ed said. "But going there? Why? Was there something he wanted to tell someone there?"

"I wish I knew." The boy's frown deepened painfully. "I was the last to see him before . . . you know. We were at the house waiting for the train to bring Dad back. He was conductor on that trip and promised to bring us all something from the city when he got back. So we was waiting and all of a sudden he said he had to go and see Chief Stockton. I didn't say anything about it. Neither did Mom. He was always saying things like that. One day he was going to fetch the mayor out of bed for something or other, then it was the President of the United States. When he said the police, we thought it was his head again. Ever since he left here—I'm sorry, Miss Yarrow but it's true—ever since he left here he was talking like that." He tapped a palm softly against the edge of the table. "I'm sorry again, Miss Yarrow, but it looks to me like it was your parents' fault for the way he was, like that. They should have kept him on, really. I mean, they gave him a good-sized going away gift, if you know what I mean. At least that's what my mother said. Enough to keep him going for a long time. But they should have kept him on. He needed that work, Miss Yarrow. Honest to God, he needed that work.

"And now he's dead. Nuts. Now he's dead."

Cyd watched helplessly as his hands embraced his cup, fell back, returned—a fierce dancing struggle against the tears he wanted to shed at his frustration and sorrow, and the image he

evidently felt he had to maintain: a boy, like a man, has no business crying. She wanted then to reach across the table to him, a
simple gesture to tell him she knew and was sorry beyond the
conventions of courtesy and form; but she kept her hands still,
clasped tightly in her lap. Either the move would be misun-
derstood, or it would be the trigger. And that she would not do
to the boy/man before her.

"It doesn't make any sense," Sandy said, poking at the cup's
handle, taking deep breaths that were released in spasms.

"It never does," Ed said. He rose after a moment, yanking up
his jacket's zipper, and stood behind him, tugging at the chair's
back. "Come on, Sandy, I'll drive you home. I don't think I'm
needed here anyway, not now." He looked over the boy's head at
Cyd, who nodded, rose herself and walked them to the door.
"I'll be in touch," he whispered as he walked outside.

Sandy turned around once on the patio, the light from the
kitchen pinning him to the night. "I'm sorry, Miss Yarrow. I just
wanted to *do* something. I just wanted to hit somebody, that's
all. I'm sorry."

She knew there should have been words for her to say to act
as a balm, but she could not find them. She only lifted a hand in
farewell instead, and watched them vanish beyond the reach of
the light. Then she turned slowly back to the room, her right
hand jumping into a fist when she saw her mother standing in
the doorway. The peasant blouse had been pulled up over her
shoulders, and one curl of grey dangled unbecomingly over her
forehead. Her face had grown taut, so much so that her lower lip
quivered until she touched a finger to it briefly without losing
her scowl.

"What were *they* doing here?"

Cyd pointed mutely at the cups on the table, too startled by
Myrtle's sudden appearance to say anything immediately.

Myrtle sniffed, raising her head slightly to jut out her chin. "I
don't like that boy," she said, then moved into the room and
walked quickly to a cupboard from which she fetched a tin of
China tea. "He tries to stir up trouble for your father and me.
Talks around the town like we're crazy or something."

"He misses his grandfather," Cyd said, surprising herself that
she automatically took the boy's defense.

"Nonsense." Myrtle spun the tin in her hands, held it tightly and tapped a long nail against its lid. "Well, I suppose that's true enough. But he says things he shouldn't. Wallace McLeod, he was old, Cynthia, very old. He wasn't as strong as he liked people to believe, the way he used to be at any rate. We couldn't keep him, that's all. Even if we could have afforded him, we couldn't keep him. I hope that's clear. Even—"

"All right, Mother, all right! He's just a boy, for heaven's sake. You'd think he'd been trying to steal the family treasure or something."

Myrtle opened her mouth to retort, apparently thought better of it and hurried to the door. At the threshold she stopped and glanced back at the table. "You invite him?"

Cyd had no answer.

Myrtle smiled. Coldly. "If you're going to stay inside, dear, you'd better take off that sweater. You'll catch your death. You are going to stay in, aren't you?"

She nodded.

Her mother nodded, as if the response were one that should be rewarded. "Well . . . as long as you're not going to prowl around anymore, I don't suppose you'd want to . . ." She lifted her shoulders in not quite a shrug.

"No, Mother, I would not. Once is enough, believe me. You grab the little creep yourself, make Father jealous. You know, sometimes I think he takes you and all that you do for granted. Why don't you let the doctor sneak you off to his clinic? It'll do Father good to get shaken now and then."

"Darling, the one thing your father does not do is take me for granted." Her smile was broad, quick, hung in the air long after she had left, as false as the statement that had caused it to spring.

"I don't believe that for a minute, Mother," she muttered to herself as she began to clean the cups from the table. And for the first few minutes she kept her mind clear as she emptied the chocolate into the sink, filled the pan and cups with hot water for soaking. But as she wiped a damp cloth over the table, she could not help seeing Sandy and the desperation on his face, the curious play of emotions that tugged hard at his lips and gave birth to an intermittent tic at the corner of one eye. It was . . .

odd. The boy was a senior at the Station high school on Steuben Avenue, his parents both commuters to an insurance firm in Hartford, and she had noticed nothing in his make-up—until now, that is—that would send him on such a fool's errand as trying to steal a car just to cause the Yarrows trouble. And the stories he was supposedly spreading around town—that was curious, too, since she had heard none of them and surely would have after all this time. The love, she thought, he must have had for that old man.

And, she added suddenly, the loyalty.

A scarce commodity in this day and age, and she wondered if she would have felt the same way had it been her own family thus afflicted.

It frightened her when a negative answer surfaced before she could stop it.

Her brothers were self-sufficient, as were her parents; and while there must have been times when she was young, times of idyllic joy and unquestionable poignancy, she understood readily that the distance of appearance-born wealth had set an almost psychic wedge between herself and the others. A wedge she could not quite put a name to but was there nevertheless. If there was loyalty, it was most likely instinctive, and not nearly as powerful as Sandy felt.

And love? She nodded to herself as she dried her hands and moved into the hall and up the stairs. Of course there was love. The family was filled with it, overflowed with it, made living here decidedly more comfortable than in most families she had seen. On the other hand, she asked herself grimly, how much of it had been demanded from history, and how much genuinely earned by the people she loved?

"Lord, Lord, aren't we getting profound in our old age," she whispered as she reached the top landing.

A sigh.

She paused, one hand still on the bannister, and looked down into the foyer. The lights in the sitting room had been turned off, the remaining guests still closeted in the dining room. She stared into the slate shadows, straining, then shrugged and took a step toward her bedroom.

*Sighing.*

The wind, she thought.

She moved across the hall and had her hand on the doorknob when she heard it again, softer, almost elusive in the dark tunnel of the corridor. She turned and walked slowly toward the front of the house, one hand out to trail along the wall, not knowing why she didn't find the nearest switch and banish the gloom.

A groan this time, and she rubbed at her arms as if chilled.

A dim light created a haze in the front hallway, spilling softly from the open door of her father's suite. She hesitated—again the reluctance to invade what had been a sanctuary—then hurried into the bedroom: large, light, with pale brown carpeting and indistinct prints on the matching walls.

Barton was lying on a broad, canopied bed, the green quilt beneath him twisted at his feet. He was naked to the waist, trousers and shoes off, eyes closed and hands clenched tightly at his sides.

"Father?" She balked at approaching him, forced herself to cross the room and lay a hand on his brow. "Father, are you all right?"

He was still, the flow of white hair pressed deeply into the pillow, the sagging of his age pulling at his shoulders and chest until he seemed to her to be more dead than alive. She drew back her hand and wiped it hard against her leg.

"Father?"

She could detect no movement, not the slightest bit of stirring. A quick glance at the door that led into his parlor, and she leaned over to place an ear against his chest. And heard nothing. Immediately, she grabbed for a wrist and fumbled to find the reassurance of a pulse. When she failed, and cursed her clumsiness, she felt the side of his neck, behind his ear, his temple . . . found nothing at all and stumbled back, away from the bed.

He couldn't be dead; she had heard him groaning.

She had.

She knew that she had.

But the longer she stared at the figure on the bed, the more she realized his chest wasn't rising, wasn't falling. And when she moved forward again, and touched a finger to an eyelid, there wasn't even the grace of a flutter.

# SIX

*People die; Yarrows do not.*

She wandered lost about the parlor, its earthen-spring colors offering no comfort in its reminders in shades of periodic resurrection.

*People die . . .*

She touched at the sidetables, at chair arms curled like lion's claws, at the books in binds of leather that were ranked behind glass fronts on the wallshelves or were tossed carelessly on cushions after brief examination. Doctor Kraylin was in the bedroom, Myrtle with him, but there was no whispering from beyond the closed door, no sudden explosions of sobbing and grief . . . and no one, after what seemed like hours, came out to reassure her, or steady her. She had wanted to get hold of Evan and Rob, but they'd left no word as to where they would be; and with Ed taking Sandy home she was far more lonely than she thought she had a right to be.

*. . . Yarrows do not.*

The house began to work on her then. Large, it became monstrous; broad, it became cavernous. Six people alone in a place built for twice that number, and she wondered why she had not long ago left for one of her own. And that, she knew, was an answer too simple to be considered seriously.

She was afraid.

Twenty-seven years stumbling through life, and she was afraid. Not of being by herself in a few small rooms of her own design; but of, at one time or another, having to come back to her family like a prodigal daughter who would rather be somewhere else and hadn't the strength. The store was her escape then, however temporary it may be. An apartment that was hers and no other's was . . . too permanent.

The fact that she knew this and understood it made her ashamed: both of the thought, and of the fact that she hadn't the courage to do much about it. At least not now. At least—

The door opened suddenly and Kraylin stepped into the room, closed the door behind him as she turned with hands clasped at her waist, eyes wide and fearful. He smiled rather briefly and without speaking walked to an ornate mahogany sideboard where he poured from a lead-topped decanter a tall, unrelieved glass of scotch. He downed it in two swallows, coughed and wiped at his eyes with the sleeve of his blazer.

"He'll be all right," he said as if he'd just realized she was there. He sagged into the nearest chair, waving her to a Victorian love seat that marked the carpet's center.

"But . . ." She fluttered her hands helplessly, not really understanding. "I mean, there wasn't a pulse, nothing. I thought he was—"

"Dead? Not quite. But for a man his age, I would say close enough."

"I don't get it. I mean, I don't understand."

"His skin color and temperature indicates to me, Miss Yarrow, what was probably a very mild heart attack."

"Oh, my God," she whispered.

"Please," he said quickly, "don't be alarmed. I only used the phrase to indicate some trouble with the heart. Don't go thinking the worst, please." The smile warmed. "I shall have him in tomorrow for a complete battery of tests just to be sure, but I'm telling you frankly there's nothing more anyone can do for him now that he can't do for himself. A night's rest is the best thing, believe me. We'll worry about what comes after later."

"Heart attack."

Kraylin's smile became surprisingly gentle. "Miss Yarrow—"

"Cyd," she corrected absently.

He nodded his thanks. "All right, I can understand your worry, and I know what that phrase sounds like: heart attack. But men like your father don't drop just like that, believe me. His biggest problem is going to be slowing down. He'll, naturally, not be able to do the work he's used to, not if he doesn't want there to be another episode like tonight's, and unless I miss my guess he's going to be an absolute holy terror around here when he gets the word." He leaned forward, hands loose on his knees. "Cyd, if you don't mind me saying so, you and I didn't quite hit it off too well down there, earlier. I know it, and I know you have an instinctive distrust of me, as well."

She squirmed on the love seat, unable to meet his gaze. "Doctor, I don't think that's entirely justified. I mean—"

"I know precisely what you mean, Cyd, and to be honest, I'm used to it. But you can rest assured that I and my staff are as well-trained and as well-qualified as anyone at the hospital. Believe me. And if I thought your father would benefit more by being there instead of in the valley, then believe me again when I say I'd have a stretcher already sitting right here in this room, ready to lug him off." He shook his head, slowly, a hand tracking up to his beard and brushing at it. "No, he's going to be fine, with the proper diet, medicine and, above all, rest."

He watched her carefully, and when she had no response he rose and dusted at his jacket until she grasped the hint and escorted him to the door. At the threshold he turned and took her hands suddenly in his. "Cyd, be sure your mother gets some sleep tonight, will you? I've left some pills on the dresser in there. Be sure that she takes two of them as soon as you can." A voice drifted down the corridor from the stairwell and he glanced toward it. "And if you wish it, I'll . . ." He gestured the rest.

Oh my God, the guests, she thought. "Yes. Yes, please, Doctor Kraylin. I don't know if I could face those who stuck around. Not right now, anyway. Just tell them . . . well, just tell them anything so they'll go. I'll get it straightened out in the morning."

"Consider it done," he said, bowed over her hands and left her watching after him.

His footsteps were swallowed the moment the light could not reach him.

And in less than an hour her father was deep in a drugged sleep, her mother beside him on the bed she had not shared with him in over a decade. Cyd stared at them closely for several minutes before she could bring herself to turn out the lights, and it was several minutes more before she was able to leave the suite for her own rooms.

But once there she found herself unable to sit or sleep, and she

threw an old woolen robe over her nightgown and began walking through the house. Her brothers had not yet returned, and
her mother had had no idea where they could have gone. A
minor debauch in the big city, she thought as she shuffled into
the kitchen and turned on the stove; boys will be boys and all
that crummy jazz.

She made herself warm milk in hopes of inducing weariness,
knew from the first sip that burned the tip of her tongue that her
nerves were far too tense for home remedies like this. It was as
though she were a cat, she thought, a cat that had seen something uncomfortable in the far corner of a room: tail puffed
slightly and the ridge of fur along the spine tingling to raise in
signal of battle. On the one hand she knew it was an appropos
image; on the other, however, she was bothered because she did
not know what had prompted it. Not all of it, at any rate.

There was admitted confusion over the matter of Cal Kraylin.
Rather stuffy when she met him first, earlier in the evening, now
she was busily rearranging her impressions to such a degree that
she nearly felt dizzy. He seemed competent enough, certainly,
and friendly, but the turnabout was so sudden and so unexpected that she almost suspected it. Shy, she told herself, or de-
fensive because he knew at once what she'd been thinking. She
shrugged. She didn't know.

And too, there was a persistent image of her father as she had
found him in his bed. Though she had no training at all in medicine, she would have sworn on any number of Bibles that he was
dead. He *had* to be, and he was not. When she had eased the
quilt up to her parents' chins before leaving them, his chest was
rising normally, and there had even been the return of a blotch
of color in each of his cheeks.

She finished the milk, rinsed out the glass and set it upside
down on the drainboard by the sink.

Color in his cheeks, and her mother with one arm thrown protectively across his stomach.

She leaned back against the counter and hugged herself
tightly, staring at the black panes in the patio door. She shook
her head and lowered her gaze to the floor.

Confusion was becoming too much a part of her life these
days.

It could all very well be the aftereffects of her bout with that idiot and his limousine, but there was still a strong, unshakable notion lurking back where she could not grab hold of it that something was wrong. No, she thought, not wrong, exactly. Not . . . wrong. But *different*. Her eyes squinted to blur her vision. It was as if, somehow, the world had decided to alter its course toward the future and had forgotten to tell her about it. Instead of looking at things one way, then another, she was still unadjusted, her eyes not quite focusing on something she knew she ought to be able to see. It was something along the lines of Poe's *The Purloined Letter* and all the imitators it had spawned over the century-plus since its creation—the answer was right there, there where she could see it without question if only . . . if . . . she shuddered. What good would it do her to recognize the answer when she did not even know what the question was?

Circles within circles and no way to pass from one to the other, she thought as she headed back toward the stairs. But at least she understood what one of her problems was—too much damned introspection. She was spending entirely too much time these days delving into the unrecognizable patterns of her own confused mind, and definitely not enough time doing something. Action. Deeds. Whatever they were, she was not doing them. And she remembered standing for an hour in the rain by the old shack, sitting in the Mariner Cove with an untouched drink in front of her . . . too much time thinking and not enough in simply *doing*. If there was in fact anything wrong—and of that too she had no proof other than some nebulous feeling, which was no proof at all—she decided she should let her subconscious gnaw on it for a while. Take her days one at a time and soon—a soon not to be measured in days or weeks—there would be an answer provided. If indeed there was an answer; if indeed there was a question to be answered.

She had her hand on the globed newel-post ready to haul her up to the first step when the telephone in the sitting room stopped her. She had no idea of the hour, save it was past midnight, but the sound of it bothered her. Strident. Demanding. All the clichés of a thousand old movies while the heroine stood at the creaky front door and debated whether or not to charge out unknowing into the trap the audience knew was there, or to pick up the receiver and be saved in the nick of time. She brushed a hand through her hair, one finger scratching at her scalp on the way, and wandered slowly across the foyer. It was most likely one of her dear absent brothers apologizing for the tardiness of their return and saying they had decided to stick around wherever they were and so would not be back until morning at the earliest. So why, she demanded silently, didn't they just wait and show up? They're big boys now, damnit.

She sighed, primed for anger. "Hello."

"Cyd, that you?" It was Ed; and the tension she had not realized she had banished returned to her arms and made them cold.

"Ed, do you have any idea what time it is? What are you—"

"I know the time, but I thought I should get to you first, before Stockton does."

Evan. Rob. She shut her eyes. "Tell me what, for God's sake."

"It's your store, Cyd. I think you'd better get yourself down here."

The cardigan sweater again, jeans, knee-boots, and a green plaid hunting jacket.

When she looked in on her parents, their sleep was still heavy and she decided not to try to wake them; the drugs they'd taken would prevent them from understanding her anyway. Instead, she rummaged through her father's dresser in the half-dark, found a sheet of stiff paper and scribbled a note on its back before laying it on the nightstand where her mother would find it should she awaken during the night. Then she was out of the house and barreling down the Pike in less than five minutes. A tight squeal around the corner at Centre Street that made her wince, a stare at the scene ahead that made her slam on her brakes.

The street was virtually dark, even for late Saturday evening. The streetlamps glowed faintly through the haze of a November mist, many of them fragmented by the arms of the trees that lined the curbs. All the neon had been extinguished, and even the distant amber globes over the Mariner Cove's doors were little more than motes that had to be stared at twice to be seen. One block down from where she had stopped, a patrol car had canted nose-in to the left-hand curbing, its rotating blue lights feeble and chilled. Beside it loomed a scarlet-and-silver truck from the mostly volunteer fire department, a helmeted man in a black slicker standing on the running board. Beyond them, on the sidewalk, a few stragglers from the cove held back by the presence of a policeman who kept his back to them, smoking a cigarette.

She began to tremble as she searched the sky and storefronts for signs of flame, signs of billowing smoke. And only when she could find nothing did she remove her foot from the brake. A moment later she parked in front of the patrol car and left her seat slowly. She refused to scream. She refused to run. A hose swelled into the bookstore, and great black ripples of water stained the concrete and fell into the gutter. There was very little of it, but to her it seemed as though her store had birthed a river.

As she walked forward, trying not to weep, a man stepped out, saw her and waited. He was wearing the same styled slicker as the man on the fire engine, but his head was bare, his hair matted and dark. She stopped, then, and he moved toward her.

I don't want to know, she thought; please, I don't want to know.

"Miss Yarrow? Cynthia Yarrow?"

She blinked slowly and refocused. He was sweating in spite of the cold, in spite of the plumes of airbreath seeping from his lips. He was tired, his face accused it, but his tone was gentle, and incongruously she thought of Calvin Kraylin.

"Miss Yarrow? You are Miss Yarrow?"

"Yes," she said quickly. "Yes, that's me." As he turned, she began to make her way on toward the door. "What . . ." She could not say it; she could only gesture.

"Near as I can make it, miss, a wire shorted in the back. In that little office thing you have there? A spark dropped into a carton stuffed with a bunch of paper." He held out his hands, palms down. "Smoldered for a long time, I imagine. Never did get a chance to get going good."

She reached the setback door and stopped again. There were spotlights inside, one on the counter and two on nearby bookcases. The carpet was stained black, and water eddied weakly about her boots. There were voices, low, and the shadows she saw flitting back and forth near the office grew until one of them paused, hurried toward her and resolved. Ed Grange called something muffled back over his shoulder, then reached out and took her arm lightly. Automatically, she stiffened to resist, thought better of it and nodded her thanks to the fireman as she was led back to her car. A staticed muttering of voices from the engine and patrol car radios; a cigarette flaring into the air, sputting in the street, flaring again and dying. A car drove north past the scene, slowed and would have stopped had not one of the policemen leaning against the hood of his vehicle waved it on.

"Is it that bad?" she said with a nod toward the shop.

Ed was without a jacket, only a heavy blue ski sweater and white corduroy trousers. On his feet, she noticed with a quick grin, were battered bedroom slippers separating in places from the age-softened soles. His hair was such a tangle she could barely resist the temptation to help it find its place.

"No," he said, "not bad at all, actually. That's why I want you to wait a minute, first, okay? If you go in there now, you'll think the place has been bombed. Those guys," and he waved toward the firemen now leaving the store, "they don't get much action around here, and when they do, they like to do things up right. It's like an accident where there's lots of blood, if you'll pardon the analogy. Better wait until the blood's gone so you can find out what the wound's really like."

"Great," she said, beginning to shiver. "Just like a cop."

"What can I say?"

They watched silently as the firemen went about their business, carting the empty boxes out onto the sidewalk and piling them at the curb where they were thoroughly doused and broken apart. She overheard one of them muttering about a frayed lamp wire, looked to Ed who nodded and shrugged. The patrolman who'd waved on the automobile earlier apparently decided she was able to answer some questions and asked her, politely, almost deferentially, for assistance with his report. When she was able to do little more than explain how she'd received word of the fire, Ed spoke up, his voice low and soft, pleasantly protective. Without realizing she was doing so, Cyd took hold of his arm as he explained he'd been having a cigarette in the small apartment he had over his office (the apartment having once

been a psychiatrist's office that had been empty for so long, he
had had no problem convincing the landlord to let him re-
model) when he saw a faint flickering glow, knew immediately
what it was and made his calls. The policeman looked up the
street then, an automatic visual check that Ed could have seen
what he'd claimed. The stores on Centre were all two-storied
and mansard roofed and, though they were all joined at street
level, the wide gaps between the roofs' double-sloped sides permitted views of the business district from the sidestreets. A quick
nod for his belief, then, a thanks to Cyd and a murmuring con-
dolence as though the shop were her child, and he was gone
with his partner who had already dispersed the few curious
onlookers.

"Sign of the times," Ed said as the patrol car backed into the
street and sped off. "Police station's right down on the corner
and they have to ride, just to make it official."

Cyd grinned, tightening her grip.

A moment later, the hose had been dragged out of the shop
and rewound on the engine. The firemen were already at their
stations and waiting impatiently as the acting captain came up to
her, his peaked hat in hand. She nodded and smiled. "Thanks,
Artie."

"Miss Yarrow, no problem, it really wasn't very much, but I
guess Ed told you that already. All that crumpled paper in the
box . . . the wire was sagging into it as much as I can figure.
You must have left it on when you went home. Mostly smoke
damage, though, and not much of that. We used less water than
it looks. Give it a day or so and a fresh coat of paint will take
care of everything." He grinned. "Of course, it'll smell like hell
for a while, but if you keep the doors and windows open, that'll
be no problem, either. And Miss Yarrow . . . next time, please
throw out all your trash right away, okay? Stick it outside in
back, in one of those dumpsters or in metal containers. I had a
date tonight, Miss Yarrow. I just hope she'll be there when I get
back."

They laughed, more from the release of tension than from the
joke, shook hands and parted. Cyd was grateful for the man's
gentleness, despite the slight scolding, and thought herself unbe-
lievably stupid for not thinking of such a simple thing as taking

care of her rubbish. Stupid, she decided, was absolutely the right word.

The engine whined, pulled away from the curb and slipped away from them silently, leaving them alone on the deserted street. The shop's open door was a cave's entrance, beckoning.

"Oh well," she said. "I better see what happened to my books." She yawned suddenly, laughed when Ed followed. "You'd better get home, pal. You look ready to drop." She walked inside quickly and switched on the overhead lights, a series of three white globes ridged and slightly greyed now by the smoke. She winced at the stains that curled like grasping fingers out from the back room up to the ceiling, but as far as she could tell none of the stock had been damaged except for a few volumes that had been knocked onto the wet carpet by the passing firemen. On her way to the office she paused for a moment, brushed a hand over Cyrano's untouched face and shook her head slowly.

And it was not until she had decided that what had to be done could easily be put off until tomorrow that she realized Ed was standing behind her. She turned and looked up at him, a sympathetic smile working her lips when she saw again the rumpled hair, the unshaven jaw, the demand for sleep in his eyes that he was denying as hard as he could.

She ignored the stench of burnt cardboard and lingering smoke, the unpleasant give of soaked carpeting beneath her feet.

"You saved my life again," she said quietly. "Sort of."

"All in a Knight's work, Lady."

She ignored, too, the pun. "Is Sandy all right?"

"As well as can be expected. He's still shook at being nabbed like that, but you've got a friend there for life, Cyd. He was really scared. Hardly said a word all the way home."

"He's a good boy. Always was. God, listen to me," she said then with a grimace. "I sound like a teacher."

A silence.

An awkwardness that soon turned her around to recheck the lock on the narrow back door—shaking her head at the firemen who'd forgotten to reset it—before following Ed to the front where she locked that door and moved out to the sidewalk. She had no idea how to leave, how to let him go after what he had done, was almost ready just to walk away when a notion made her stop in the middle of a stride. "Wait a minute," she said. "How did you know it was my store, anyway? And how did they get in there without smashing anything?"

Ed looked up at the nightsky and cleared his throat, folded his arms over his chest, dropped them, stuffed his hands into his pockets. He took two steps from her toward the curb to open her car door, but she grabbed his arm and held him tightly.

"Edwin Grange, what have you been up to behind my back?"

"A lovely back, I must say. One of the nicest, in fact, that—"

"Ed!"

It was one of her mother's favorite and oft-used axioms that every male had within his repertoire of begging expressions the standard little boy plea: *Don't hurt me, Mommy, I was only trying to help.* But she'd thought that Ed, of all people, would have long since abandoned such an obvious ploy. Not this time, however. His right hand remained in his trouser pocket while his left scratched at his cheek, temple, into his hair and down to his nape while his face contorted into what seemed like a permanent grimace. Both hand and a foot in the cookie jar, she decided; but she waited to see if she had a right to be angry.

"Ed," she prompted softly, the tone suggesting she wouldn't spank him.

"Angus," he said finally, his voice hoarse until he cleared his throat. He checked the sky again, glanced in the direction of his apartment's safety. "I keep a file of store owners, you know, hit them every so often with one of my brochures for security guards, alarm systems, things like that. When I saw that carpenter go in there last week, I knew someone was getting ready to move in. So I asked around, Angus told me."

"Well, why didn't you tell me that you knew?"

"I figured you didn't want anybody to know. You wanted me to know, you'd tell me in your own good time. I know you, Cyd. I could wait."

"And the key?" Immediately, she held up a hand. "Don't tell me—Angus. Keep an eye on the poor girl, Eddie," she said, mimicking the lawyer's deep-throated Harvard accent. "She's a fine one, she is, but she doesn't know her butt from a beetle sometimes."

Ed released a long and loud sigh, nodded and sheepishly pulled the key from his pocket. He tossed it in the air and she snatched at it, stared at it, then set it firmly in his palm. "I would have given you one, you know. I'm too nervous, even with the cops just down around the corner. Have you . . . I mean, did you—"

"No," he said. "I haven't been in there once, not once. No reason to. Angus figured you might do something stupid like leave cash in a drawer after hours, you see. I was going to check around the first few nights after you opened just to be sure you were on the ball."

"Oh, you were, huh?"

"I were, yes."

She grabbed his shoulders and kissed him quickly on the cheek. Stared at him for what seemed like the reading of a lifetime, and kissed his lips. Slowly. Gently. Pulled away before his hands could move to her back.

"If you have nothing better to do tomorrow," she said, "I have some cleaning in there."

"I don't moonlight."

"In broad daylight, you idiot. I'm not proud."

# SEVEN

Too fast, Cyd thought as she skirted close to panic, but it was, finally, too late to do anything about it. The shop had opened and the aisles, if not crowded, were at least reasonably traveled. Whatever she had forgotten—and there had to be something—would have to wait until she'd won the struggle with her nerves to keep herself from screaming.

The cleanup following the Sunday fire had gone quickly, almost too quickly. When she arrived in town shortly before noon both Ed and Sandy were waiting for her at the curb, pails and buckets, brushes and brooms stacked against the shop windows while they listened intently to Sandy's transistor radio. Before she had a chance to designate chores and set her priorities, they had already begun, paying her no mind and more often than not driving her into the back room where she hid, gratefully, from their labors. By supper it was done and, as had been predicted, there was only a faint smell left to leave a clue to the accident.

On Monday, Paul ambled by in a worn overcoat and his crimson scarf, hands deep in his pockets and his eyes on the rooftops as he tried to appear casual. Cyd had grinned, had let him in, and had watched in amazement as he'd handled the newly arrived heavy cartons as though they were empty, studied the carpeting and ran off to fetch runners to hide the dark stains.

Iris joined him on Wednesday, and it was then that Cyd began to wonder what she was going to do in such a small shop with two eager assistants. It did not take long for her apprehension to fade: while Paul busied himself learning title locations for quick, efficient answers, Iris discovered the ledgers Cyd had prepared for the accounting, found also a half-dozen errors that would have had them all working well past midnight most nights of the week.

"You," Cyd said without a second thought, "are hereby my manager."

Iris only grinned.

The biggest surprise was Sandy McLeod. After insisting that he knew a lot more about books than it seemed by his grades, he had smiled and cajoled his way into a two-nights-a-week-and-full-time-Saturday job. Nodding toward the Lennons, who had been huddled over something in back, he'd said, "They're going to get tired, you know, Miss Yarrow. And you really can't do it all by yourself, right?"

Ed installed an alarm system, both burglar and fire.

And two weeks to the day before Christmas, after the first ads in the *Station Herald* had announced the grand opening, she unlocked the door and stepped quickly behind the counter. Palms moist, stomach lurching, while Paul sat on the high stool behind the register and checked once again the mechanics of its working. Though Cyd had to admit the new machine was quiet, pronounced change to be made and automatically computed the state sales tax, she wished she could hear the harsh punch of old keys, the slide of the drawer and the announcement of the metallic bell that a sale had been made.

Iris sat in back, in a new print dress and a gauze-thin scarf, clucking at salesmen's brochures, once exclaiming aloud at the lurid description of a new historical romance.

An hour passed, and no one walked in.

"Relax," Paul said when, for the dozenth time, she backed out to the sidewalk and studied the two window displays for errors or offense. As in the other windows on Centre Street, just a delicate touch of Christmas—no flashing lights, nothing distasteful or garish. "They'll come. They have the money they'll come." He sniffed and jammed a well-chewed, chipped pipe into his mouth, lit it and forgot it.

*Yarrow's.*

She stared at the letters. No mention of books. Only her name. It had been Rob's idea, seconded by Evan. They had come the day before to help her doublecheck for the opening, had been quiet enough in their prowling of the aisles, touching here, finger-dusting there until they'd announced their satisfaction and prepared to leave.

"But what do I call it?" she'd asked in despair.

"What's the matter with 'Yarrow's'?" Rob said.

"What? But that's so . . . I don't know . . . it doesn't have . . . I don't know!"

Evan almost grinned. "Listen, Cyd, there's no need to be fancy in the Station, you know that. Just give it your name, like Rob says. People read the paper, they know what you're selling."

"Not a bad location, either," his brother had said solemnly. "The bank next door is perfect. People make withdrawals and head up the street, decide to drop in for a look around and the next thing you know their envelopes are thinner."

"Shrewd girl," said Evan.

"My sister," said Rob.

She'd worked past midnight with stencils and paint. Simple letters in simple proclamation.

And just before noon the first customer walked in: Mrs. Angela Harper in her furs, white gloves, and a perpetual scowl. Cyd smiled as she greeted her and was about to join her when Paul took hold of her arm gently and kept her behind the counter.

"Miss Yarrow," he said, with one eye on the old woman who had stalked immediately to the Gothics, "a word with you, please."

"Can't it wait, Paul? My God, this could be my first sale. Ever. Do you know what that means?"

"You ain't never been a servant, Missy. I have. Never dog the folks you work for. They need, they'll ask. You just watch their faces. They're afraid to ask, you just stand around a bit, just in range, and they'll get the nerve up. But don't dog them, Missy, don't dog them."

An hour later she was fighting her panic: "They're not buying, Iris!"

"Miss Yarrow, they're more curious now than charitable. What's a rich girl doing working a place like this they want to know. Did she go broke and we don't know it? She get herself tossed out on her ear? They're looking for gossip, Missy, a little bit of dirt. But don't you worry. Bookstores is like something ain't never been in the world—almost impossible to walk in and walk out without buying something. Even if you don't need it.

It's guilt. You feel funny coming out empty-handed. Guilt. Don't worry, you ain't going broke."

"How are we doing, Paul?"
"You ask me that one more time, Missy, and I'm quitting."

Dale and Victor Blake came in behind a huge bouquet of flowers, dragged her off to the luncheonette for something to eat, and never stopped laughing.

"Paul—"
"Miss Yarrow, why don't you take a walk or something?"

By midafternoon the shop was empty again, and she moved slowly past the shelves, rearranging those titles shifted out of place, gathering the inventory cards that had been dropped on the floor. She searched for patterns of sale and rejection, found a few and scribbled on a pad she kept in her hand. As she drifted past the office she saw Iris bending over a low pile of order forms, sorting out the requests that had come her way once she had had the foresight to tack a "Special Orders" sign on the jamb near her desk. The woman sensed her, looked up and smiled curtly, returned to her work as though it were Cyd and not she who constituted the help. Paul was still at the register, smoking thoughtfully and watching the traffic.

I don't believe this, she thought, straightening a low cardboard display rack in a far corner. The fear that had assaulted her at the sight of Mrs. Harper had quickly faded to the nervousness that had made Paul irritable; from there she'd sidled into a numbing calm, her smile automatic, her answers to idle questions courteous and sincere but brooking no conversation beyond a few moments. She knew as she spoke that her manner still left much to be desired, but she had been unable to establish a solid contact between the real world, the world of her shop, and the people who inhabited both. By the time it was four, however, she hoped she was normal again. Not once did she head for the sidewalk, nor did she fuss with the displays or count the cash in the drawer. She left Iris alone, stopped staring at the pedestrians trying to will them in like a psychic spider to vulnerable flies, instead picked up a volume of Yeats' poetry and immediately fell into the lyric melancholy that marked his *Easter Rebellion* stanzas and the eulogies they whispered. She barely noticed when someone stepped up behind her and poked a hard thumb at her shoulder.

"Yes?"

"You got any good stuff, lady? Porno, stuff like that?"

She froze, suddenly recognized the voice and shook her head. "You want degradation, mister, you'll have to watch TV." She replaced the book, turned and grinned, instantly felt her eyes brimming and cursed herself roundly.

Ed glanced around the aisles in slow examination. "Looks like a hurricane hit the place. I take it that's a good sign."

"I hope so," she said.

His voice softened. "You look tired."

She was about to play her courage role and deny it as vehemently as she thought Ed would stand it, then sagged against a wall shelf and pushed a hand through her hair. "Tired is not the word for it, sir. I feel like I've been trampled by a herd of elephants, and the doctors left me on the table and forgot to put me back together again. Does that make sense?" She frowned. "I don't care. Yes, Ed, I am tired."

"Then how about some dinner?"

Her eyes widened and her gaze darted about the shop. "Oh, I can't, Ed, really. Do you see this place? I mean, I'm staying open until nine all week, do you know what that means? Really, I don't think I can—"

He pressed a palm against her mouth until, playfully, she tried to bite him. "All right," he said. "Paul isn't stupid, and neither is Iris. They work for you, remember? And you'll only be gone for an hour, I promise. And I also promise the store will still be here when we get back, okay?"

"But Ed—"

He grinned and dropped an arm around her shoulder, led her to the front. "Cyd, I know you, remember? I know your type. You're a fine manager, a great organizer, you'd make one hell of an executive if someone gave you the chance. But you'll be dead before the new year if you don't learn quick to delegate some of the responsibility now and then. Look, today you're tired more because of nerves than anything else. Tomorrow you'll be tired because you're being slightly dumb."

"Slightly . . ." She looked over to Paul, who immediately began refilling his pipe. She knew he was right, especially since he'd shifted her concentration from the shop to her stomach and she discovered the hollow. She knew he was right, yet . . . she watched Paul studying a spot on the register, nodded and hurried back to the office to fetch her coat from the rack. Iris looked up, her glasses perched on her forehead like a second pair of eyes disturbingly transparent.

"Dinner?" she said.

Cyd nodded. "I'll be an hour, no more. Then you and Paul—"

"No matter," Iris said, reaching under the desk to show her a brown shopping bag piled with sandwiches wrapped in wax paper. "We'll eat when we're ready, Missy. We don't have regular hours at home, we don't expect them here for a while."

Cyd smiled, reached out to turn up the bulb in the desk lamp. The switch clicked over twice, once more to turn the light on again. "Nuts. I'll have to stop at the drug store and get a new one. It should be three-way. You can't work in light like this, Iris, it'll ruin your eyes."

"Oh, I don't mind."

"Iris, don't argue."

The old woman glanced up, mildly shocked despite the quivering lips that traced a smile. "You do the boss part very well, Missy."

"Oh, I try, Iris, I try."

But it wasn't until she and Ed had reached the corner on their way to the Cove when suddenly she stopped, a hand on his arm. Looking back over her shoulder, she stared at the storefront.

"What is it, Cyd? You forget something?"

It was already dark, the streetlamps on to add to the neon. Traffic, for Oxrun, was mildly heavy as offices emptied and late shoppers did their chores. A patrol car slipped by, a long and dark taxi. A yellow school bus filled with noise and cheerleaders and the basketball team. The scent of moisture in the air. The promise of a frost.

"Oh my God," she said. "I don't believe it."

"What?" he said.

"I'm not sure yet. Let me think."

They found a small booth near the kitchen door in the Cove's restaurant, a room the same size as the adjoining lounge but twice as crowded with tables for diners. And though there were already several families with children the noise level was low, almost intolerably so. Cyd said nothing, waiting until they had ordered and the order had arrived before she launched into what she knew beforehand was a meaningless prattling about the shop's first day and the fears she had had of somehow offending a customer and not making a dime. Ed listened to her carefully, ate as quickly, made her increasingly uneasy by his too-thoughtful staring, and the muttered comments and compliments that came unerringly in exactly the right places. He knows I'm stalling, she thought in a panic, and she began to speak faster, stumbling over her words and forgetting her place until, finally, he snapped out a hand to lay on her wrist.

"Quiet," he said, and pointed with his fork. "Eat that damned scrod before it gets cold. Then you can tell me what's going on."

"I don't know," she said. "I don't know if anything's going on."

"Yes, you do," he said, disturbingly accurate. "Eat."

"Damned peasants," she muttered as she picked up her knife. "Never know their place."

But she ate nonetheless, mechanically, tasting little as she tried to make sense of what was invading her mind. And when the dishes had been cleared and the sherry served in fragile clear glasses, she leaned back into the booth's corner and stared over his head.

"The lamp," she said. "The car. You ever get the feeling someone's trying to get you?"

Ed lit a cigarette, blew the smoke to one side. "One thing at a time, all right? Yes, I do get that feeling someone's after me, but in my case that's generally true—at least it was when I was a cop around here. The car—if you mean that idiot who nearly squashed you last month, I understand. But what does the lamp have to do with anything?"

"The afternoon of the fire I was in the store," she said, the words coming slowly as she took deep breaths for calming. "I had the lamp on the counter so I could see what I was doing. Ed, I did not move it back to the office. I wasn't back there working that day. And the cartons, they were piled up against the back wall, not by the desk." She held up a hand to stop him from interrupting. "That lamp came from my room at home, and I'll bet a million of Father's dollars that the wire wasn't frayed. How could it be? I just bought it recently." She stared at his cigarette, at the hypnotic amber tip. "It never occurred to me. The excitement, the police, you . . . it just went out of my mind I was so worried about the store."

Ed took a slow, deliberate sip of his sherry. "You trying to make a connection between that fool kid and his car, and the fire?"

"The fire was set, Ed, I'll swear to it."

Slowly he placed his glass in front of him, not looking at her, his fingers lightly tapping the thin stem until she wanted to snatch the glass away. A minute passed in century time before he snapped his fingers for the waitress, handed her a twenty-dollar bill for the check and slid out of the booth. "This is no place to talk about something like that," he said, holding out one hand until she took it and joined him. "I think we need to take a long, slow walk. And don't," he said as the double doors hissed closed behind them, "worry about the store. I'll get you back in time."

"Ed, we're going to freeze!" she protested as he steered them across the street and right, heading for the park. With one hand she bunched her camel's-hair coat at the throat while the other fisted in her pocket.

"You'll also think more clearly," he said. "Come on, step it out, Cyd. Think for a while more, then talk. Say one word before you're ready, and you'll only confuse yourself."

The park was enclosed by a tall, spike-topped fence of black iron; the sidewalk broadened into a concrete apron in front of the matching gates, and Ed scowled when he saw the thick-linked chain woven through the fence and around the lock.

Beyond, there was nothing but still, winter black.

"Good idea," she said when he shook the gates in frustration. "What do you do now, climb over and haul me up by the hair?"

"I never said I was perfect," he growled.

"You," she said, "must have been one heck of a cop."

He darted a playful hand toward the shock swept over her forehead. "Too short," he said. "You'd make a lousy Rapunzel."

A van sped past them, honked once, and a young girl's laugh hung coldly in the air.

"Oh well," he said, waited until she had linked her arm with his, then began walking slowly down Park Street, back toward Chancellor. They kept their heads down, watching their breath vanish as fast as it puffed white. Oxrun was silent then, and Cyd stayed off her heels so not to disturb it.

"I don't know," she said finally. "I don't think I know."

"Know what?"

"I don't know if they're connected, the fire and the car. But they must be, Ed. That fire was deliberate, and the limousine was no accident, no matter what you and Father say." She stopped, pulling him around to face her; her limbs grew colder, and the December night grew as if ready to swallow her. "Tell me I'm crazy, but it sounds like someone's trying to kill me."

"No," he said immediately. "No, not quite."

"But Ed—"

He forced her to walk again, to listen to the crack of his shoes on the sidewalk, the cars whispering past as they angled away from the park and its black iron teeth. A nightbird called, was answered and called again; a pair of buff cats sped out from beneath a hedge, spotted them, veered sharply to retrace their flight; a radio, muffled; and Cyd began to debate on what the store had done to her mind, and her thinking, and her perception of what was real.

Two blocks later they were at the corner, standing beneath an ornamental streetlamp whose two globes were crackling dim. They saw a group of men and women leave the Mariner Cove, huddle on the sidewalk before heading off toward the Inn; probably, she thought, to take advantage of the music featured five nights a week.

Ed coughed, and she jumped. She did not smile.

"Listen, Cyd," he said with his chin tucked into his dark coat, "if someone was trying to kill you, it would have been done already. By that car if nothing else, but it didn't happen again, did it? You were brushed back—"

"You call that brushed back?"

"—and you were chased. Not a damn thing else. The fire, too, was very carefully set—*if*, mind you, *if* that's true. And if it is, then whoever set it made sure it would be a smoldering one, not something akin to an explosive spreading. If it's true, whoever did it wanted damage, not death. Remember, it happened when you weren't even there, so late at night that nobody possibly could have been there.

"I don't know. It's a lot of conjecture, obviously, but I really think, Cyd, you've made a connection over two things that happened nearly three weeks apart." His smile, then, was gentle. "No offense, but I think you're reaching."

"Ed, the lamp . . . was not in the back room."

"Are you sure?"

"I just said so, didn't I?"

The smile grew and his hands took her elbows. "My dear lady, if you think hard enough you'll probably remember that you were rather excited at the time, planning the ads and the opening, getting the Lennons to work for you, things like that. It would have been very easy for you to stop work, for instance, and just pick up the lamp and carry it back into the office out of the way. An automatic thing, see? Something you might not remember even if you were shown a picture of it."

It made sense. It could have been true. It could be true now. She put a hand over her eyes as though blocking her vision would flush out the answer.

"M'dear," he added, "lamps do not fly."

"Now that much," she said, "I'll grant you in a minute. You know, this is all very confusing. As if I didn't have enough troubles these days, I don't need this, too. But maybe you're right, maybe it is the day. You know what I mean: the shop opening and all this excitement and my nerves and people not coming in until almost lunchtime, which drove me right up the wall, believe me." She rubbed hard at the back of her neck, looked up at him ruefully. "But I still—"

"Come on, Cyd!"

"No, really, Ed, listen for a minute. I know that what you say has got to be true. I mean, who would want to kill me? Who would even want to hurt me? The fire . . . it could be someone, I don't know, someone who didn't want competition, even

though there isn't another bookstore for miles around here. Or
maybe it's someone who wants the location bad enough that
they're trying to scare me off. I don't know. Does that make
sense? And what does that stuff have to do with the car?"

"Cyd, now you're confusing me."

She laughed, snapped her fingers and dug into her pockets.
"Wait a minute. Bear with me just one more minute, okay? A
list, that's what I need. I always make a list whenever I start
confusing myself about one thing or another. It's compulsive I
guess. And how did I get this thing?"

She held up a handkerchief, crumpled and white, and stared
at it, at Ed, who only shrugged and flicked it with one finger.

"Oh. Yeah, now I remember. A few days ago Mother cut her
finger on a piece of broken glass. She wrapped this thing around
it. I think it was the day I went to see Iris and Paul about the
store. Maybe the next day, I don't remember. When I got back,
it was on the dining room table. I just picked it up and stuffed it
in my pocket."

"Pack rat," he said.

"Could be worse. Here," and she pulled out a sheet of paper
folded in quarters. "Pack rat," she agreed with a smile. "Beats
carrying a purse sometimes, though it gets just as crowded in
here. You got a pen, pencil?"

His bemusement increased as he slipped his hand into his
coat, then shrugged when he came up with nothing.

"Some cop," she muttered as she unfolded the paper. "I
thought you guys were always supposed to be . . . what in
heaven's name is this?"

"How should I know?" he said. "I haven't got X-ray vision."

She held it up to the light. "Would you believe it's the note I
wrote for my folks that same night, the night of the fire? I must
have . . ." She turned the paper over, back . . . and her hand
froze. A long second later Ed slipped the paper from her fingers,
and she barely felt the loss, barely heard his curse when he read
what she had.

"It's a joke," he said. "What else can it be?"

Cyd was not sure; she wasn't sure of anything anymore. If it
was a joke, it was one in exceedingly poor taste. And if not . . .
it was meaningless.

"It's . . ."

"I know," he said. "I know what it is, I've seen plenty of them. In fact, it's from Oxrun, though I don't know how he got hold of one."

"Ridiculous," she said, trying to rally. "What would he be doing with a damned death certificate?"

The date on the form was June 23; the name on the form was Barton Quincy Yarrow.

# EIGHT

The evening moved slowly. Voices droned as from a run-down Victrola while the air grew gel-thick and extraordinarily warm. Several times Cyd caught Iris looking at her strangely, her expression clouded with an unformed question not her place to ask. There were customers, many of them and buying, and she fought to keep her smile so not to frighten them away. Ed was gone, returned to his office to close it for the night. And by the time he had returned and was chatting with Paul, the first day of her dream had finally ended.

At nine o'clock the door shade was pulled down.

At nine-thirty, the Lennons left with flowers and congratulations and a kiss each for her cheek.

And as soon as the door closed, Cyd slumped against the counter and spread the certificate beneath her hands. Stared at it, examined it, twisted it around until she was sure it would not change.

"If you thought I was confused before," she said with a false, high laugh, "you ought to see inside me now."

"Hey," Ed said softly, standing beside her, one elbow on the register, a palm to his cheek. "Hey, Cyd, you know it's a gag. I mean, your father's home right now, recovering from a heart attack."

"It says here that's what he died from."

Ed closed his eyes, slowly. "Cyd, I don't know what your problem is—"

"Then you haven't been listening."

"—but this," and he slapped at the paper, "is a joke, okay? A lousy, miserable joke. And if you don't mind me saying so, it sounds like something your brothers would cook up."

Cyd denied it instantly. Evan and Rob, though they had their light moments, were far too conservative, bound far too deeply in the staid world of finance to consider even remotely something that was too evidently in such poor taste. Yet, when Ed insisted, she reluctantly admitted that if it had to be one of them it would probably be Evan. Rob, too much like her father, didn't even know a limerick, scarcely knew how to smile. Again, however, she dismissed the notion, moved to the nearest rack and picked up a book, flipped idly through the pages before replacing it, upside down. She reached then for another, but Ed took hold of her shoulders, turned her around and sat her on the stool. She did not protest.

"We do this logically and slowly," he said through a deep breath. "Good Lord, you're going to drive yourself into hysteria if you're not careful." He waited. She said nothing. "Good. Now then, let's go back to the beginning, from what you told me before.

"First, we know you got the paper from your father's room, right? Right. Exactly where did you find it?" He held up a cautioning finger. "Slowly, understand."

"All right." Her hands were clasped tightly in her lap, broke apart and began toying with the buttons on her blouse. "They were sleeping, Mother and Father, and when you called I didn't want them to worry if they woke up and found no one in the house. I don't know where Evan and Rob were. So I grabbed something out of Father's dresser, wrote the note on it and left. The next morning I was straightening up—they were still sleeping—and I must have shoved the paper into my coat. I—" She stared at him, trying to read his expression. "Oh my God, it was Father."

Ed shrugged, "It had to be. He got the form from somewhere, and for him it would be easy, and probably thought it would be funny to fill it out. Obviously, nobody was supposed to find it. He probably didn't even remember he had it."

"But why June 23?"

Ed picked up a ball-point and began doodling in the margins. "Beats me. When . . . when was he ill?"

Cyd nodded quickly. "Yes. Sure. I was in . . . I don't know, Italy, I think . . . and he had to go back to Kraylin's place because that pneumonia wouldn't quit on him. As I understand it, he was in and out most of the month. I almost came home, but Mother wouldn't hear of it." She pulled her purse from beneath the counter and carefully placed the certificate inside. "Poor Father. It may have been a joke, but I wonder if he thought he was really going to die?"

There was almost a hint of a tear in her eye before she sniffed the possibility back and busied herself with the closing. The day's receipts she placed in a canvas bank sack, wrapping it tightly with an attached leather-and-metal cord. The change remaining for the next day's use she locked in a small safe set in the bottom of the office filing cabinet. Then she activated the alarms Ed had installed, switched off the lights and ushered him out with a gentle push. When the street door was secured she stepped back to the sidewalk and looked at the shop carefully, critically, before nodding.

And crying.

No sobs. Her shoulders remained still. But the tears dampened her cheeks unashamedly, and Ed stayed to one side, counting leaves in the gutter.

When she was done she blew her nose noisily, shook her head once and stepped quickly to the bank where she dropped the sack into the night-deposit slot.

From somewhere in the distance, the sound of a carol to remind her of the season.

"You need a ride?"

She looked up the street as if it were the first time she'd seen it. "As a matter of fact, Rob was supposed to pick me up half an hour ago. I guess he forgot."

Ed's car was still parked by his office, and they walked there slowly, as slowly as they could, and by the time they reached the corner his arm was around her waist. There was nothing to be said, and nothing needed to be said. It was a moment Cyd knew was all too rare: when friends not necessarily lovers conversed with their silence.

They rode almost as slowly, almost as quietly, Cyd only once making a joke about the car phone and Ed not responding. And when she asked to be let off at the front of the drive he made a swift U-turn and reached across her to open the door. Kissed her lightly, with a grin for congratulations.

"Have a good rest," he whispered as she slid out, and she stood there watching the taillights wink and disappear as they took the gentle curve back to the Station. Then she hunched her shoulders against the night breeze and kicked at a twig. If you're not more careful, my dear, she told herself as she walked, that kind of man could get to be a habit.

She grinned, lifted her face to the air and whistled; a medley of tunes only a few bars each. And here, in the dark of the lane with the spiderleg trees waiting overhead, even the idea of the fire seemed somehow too distant. There was still the conviction that it had been deliberately set, but she refused to allow the thought to dispell her current mood. There were any number of possible explanations for it—from the innocent to the macabre—but they could wait until tomorrow, when she talked with Abe Stockton. She blinked. Until the moment the name popped into her head she had had no thought at all of seeing the Chief of Police. But it had to be done. No doubt it was too late to do anything about the fire now, but at least her complaint would have been noted in case it happened again.

The trees parted, the house loomed, and she saw the shades drawn in the living room, figures moving behind them sporadically and—she frowned—apparently angry. She hurried to the front door and listened a moment before letting herself in.

"I don't care what you say, damnit! I want the thing found, and I want it found now!"

Her brother's voice filled the house with thunder, sparked the lamps with lightning. She had not heard such a temper in over a decade, not since the year a California conglomerate had tried to buy the family out with an offer each one of them had considered insulting.

"Now Robert—"

"Now nothing, Mother." His voice was lower now, and more dangerous. Cyd moved to the doorway and looked in, half expecting to see Rob wearing full armour. Her parents were sitting in armchairs that faced the fireplace television, Evan was standing at the far, darker side of the room studying intently the portraits on the wall. Rob was on the hearth, blocking the screen. When he saw her, he worked at a smile, and Barton rose as soon as she entered, extending a hand that she took firmly to push him back down.

"I don't know what you're all yelling about," she said, glaring at Rob until he moved several paces away, "but you, dear old Dad, are not supposed to be out of bed."

Barton scowled, pushing himself deeper into the cushions like a scolded child. "Fools for children, fools for partners," he muttered with a jerk of his thumb toward his eldest son. "Fifteen years he works for me, I taught him everything I know, and he dares blame me for misplacing a contract. One lousy contract," he said, louder.

"It is important," Rob said, watching his brother approach them almost cautiously.

"Damnit—"

"Enough, the both of you!" Cyd said. "You're both being silly."

"Your father's upset, dear," Myrtle said, a glass in her hand. "He wouldn't stay in bed, so I let him come down to watch the basketball game. Just for a minute. I didn't think it would do any harm. Then your brother came home, and he and your father . . ." She spread her hands as though the rest were obvious.

"You have a television in your bedroom," Cyd reminded him with a poke to his shoulder.

"Screen's bigger down here," Barton muttered.

"Oh, for heaven's sake, Father, do you want to kill yourself?" She started to laugh, cut herself off when she saw the look on her mother's face—shock, disbelief; and for one curious moment she thought she had seen that expression before. She shook it off quickly with a false, high cough, and wondered aloud if anyone cared how her first day had gone. Immediately, gratefully, she was surrounded, inundated with questions she tried to answer as best she could. In the middle of the storm Rob vanished for several minutes, returned with a pewter tray, glasses of champagne, and a wedge of Barton's favorite Dutch cheese. Cyd laughed, felt the tears again, but this time wiped at them quickly with the backs of her hands. Then they toasted her boisterously, and Barton launched into a history of his own commercial start, the competitors he faced and defeated, the competitors he faced and absorbed. Myrtle corrected him on several occasions, but did it so gently that no one paid her any mind.

The cheese was consumed. Another wedge. More wine, until Rob sliced through the heel of his thumb and the sight of the blood on the cutting board quieted them, eventually sent them all to bed.

Midnight, and Cyd sat on the edge of her mattress, sorry she had drunk so much, reminding herself mock-sternly that she was a working woman now and needed to keep reasonably decent hours.

But it had been glorious, the only word for it.

All the panic, the upset, the fears and the errors had all been worth it because it did not matter now whether she made it or not. For once in her life she had taken a major step without Barton's tall shadow covering hers, and the money ready to cushion her fall, and the excuses ready for the press if they were needed. She had done it. On her own. She had survived the first day without falling apart.

She applauded herself and giggled, hiccoughed, giggled again and decided it was time to revive an old custom. Before she lost her nerve she slipped into a robe and hurried out of her rooms. Stumbled over her shadow and covered her mouth with one hand. You're drunk, my dear, she told herself as she collided with the wall; you're drunk and you don't care, do you?

By the time she had worked her way around the staircase to the front, she thought she had made enough noise to wake the whole house, but there were no lights glowing, no sounds beyond the doors when she pressed an ear to them.

*Something.*

She grabbed hold of the railing around the stairwell and stared into the dark.

*Something.*

She closed her eyes, hoping to clear her head, succeeding only in making herself dizzy. Her legs trembled, her arms quivered, and she swallowed in a panic to keep herself from vomiting.

But there was *something* in the house, *something* in the hallway that alerted her to a sensation quite close to danger.

She wanted to call out, changed her mind and hand over hand pulled herself to the rear of the house where she stopped in the center of the corridor and looked ahead, looked behind, half expecting one of her brothers to come lurching out of his room, as drunk as she and twice as full of mischief.

She hiccoughed. Belched. Felt acid rise in her throat, and a feeling of disgust that made her grimace.

There was no danger. There was no . . . *something*. There was only the wine and the bubbles and the emotional letdown from the high of the shop's opening day. She sagged. Slumped. Looked over her shoulder quickly, just to be sure, then used the wall for a brace and pulled herself to her feet.

"F-fool," she muttered as she nearly fell into her parlor, tripped over a chair leg and slammed her shoulder against the jamb. "Idiot," she snapped, wandered into the bathroom where she splashed cold water on her face, the back of her neck, until the shivering cleared her mind somewhat and she stumbled into bed.

Dreaming of bloodred cheese and bloodred smiles.

Dreaming of shadows against shadows that prowled the hallways, sniffing, searching, prodding, poking, until they burst into her family's rooms and smothered them screaming.

Dreaming of cash registers overflowing with money, rooms filled with dimes and nickels and quarters, stores like her own bulging at the seams with grey canvas sacks that held millions of dollars. While Iris and Paul helped her in the counting, and Sandy and Ed danced with her till dawn.

Dreaming.

And waking.

Tuesday, the second day.

Thursday morning she was anxious to get started early. Iris had begun the day before to complain of an impending cold, and she did not want to force the old woman into work if she could help it. At Iris' age, she thought as she rushed through a breakfast of coffee and tepid toast, the slightest lung problems could mean potential disaster. Better she be first for a change, call Paul and see if she could persuade him to leave his wife home.

When she was done and the dishes piled in the sink, she darted into the hallway struggling into her coat. It was a green cloth affair she had found in her wardrobe, one she had forgotten but one she had decided was much better than the camel's hair; less pretentious, less blatant, certainly more fitting. She grinned as she shook her head at herself, stopped when her casual glance swept past the library door, reversed itself and made contact.

The door was open. She frowned, wondering if her father had renewed an old habit and had fallen asleep in one of his chairs while reading. She had a feeling that, despite his attack and Kraylin's orders, no one could keep him still for more than a few days. With a stern expression, then, she stepped into the vast room, a command on her lips that soon died. The french doors to the veranda were open all the way, the morning breeze teasing the white curtains. And on the left-hand wall the six-foot portrait of her paternal grandfather had been shoved to one side on its top-frame hinges, and the wall safe gaped in the first glow of morning.

For several moments she was unable to speak, to breathe, to do more than stare. Then she screamed for her father. For Evan. For Rob. Screamed louder, and was bracing to race upstairs when her parents in their bathrobes met her at the threshold. Cyd babbled hysterically, then pointed while Barton looked inside, returned grim-faced and was reaching for the wall phone extension by the kitchen door when Rob joined them.

"Rob—"

He pushed through them and stood on the edge of the oriental carpet. Nodded. Walked over to the doors and closed them, opened them, nodded once again. Then he crossed to the safe and peered in.

"Well, isn't anyone going to say anything?" Cyd demanded, everything inside her telling her to start yelling again. "For God's sake, do you want me to call the police?"

"No," Barton said.

Cyd thought she heard him incorrectly. "Father, listen to me: There's been a robbery. Mother's jewels," and she turned to her mother who only took her arm and held on.

"Darling," she said, "there's no sense, really. They're not marked or anything like that, they're diamonds for the most part." She nodded toward the doors. "Isn't it obvious? The thief knew what he was doing. Probably one of my dear friends' friends we had over the other night. He took a walk around, saw what he wanted and came back while we were sleeping. He's long gone now. He'll never be caught."

"They cut the diamonds and things out of the settings, Cyd," Evan said, still in his pajamas and coming up behind her. "Then they can sell them and no one knows the difference."

Cyd yanked her arm free, looked from one face to another. "I don't believe this," she said. "I don't know how many thousands of dollars' worth of stuff has been taken from your very own house, and all you people can do is tell me that you're not going to report it." She glanced into the corridor, turned back and nearly shouted, "Well, if you don't call Stockton, damnit, then I will!"

Everyone tried speaking at once, no voice dominating until Cyd clamped her hands over her ears, waited until Rob took hold of his mother's arm as she had her daughter's. "Cyd's right, you know," he said, so quietly they all had to stop in order to hear him. "As usual, she's right." He smiled down at his mother. "You're forgetting something, aren't you? The insurance. There's no way we can collect a dime unless it's reported to Abe."

Thank God, there's someone still sane around here, she thought; and leave it to Rob to know what to do.

Barton seemed as if he were going to argue on, then sagged as though he were a deflated balloon. "You're right, son," he said, almost sighing. He looked then to Cyd, a weak smile at his lips. "I'm sorry, dear, but . . . well, this has never happened to us before. It's just a reflex, I suppose. You know what I mean—keep it in the family, we can handle it ourselves. Legacy of your grandfather I suspect it is."

"Pride is what you're talking about," she said, more angrily than she had intended, but not sorry for it. "But for God's sake, Father, pride or not this is a crime you're talking about here, not some damned company trying to take you over. And if you've got money problems—"

"Who told you that?" Evan demanded.

She looked at him in disgust, turned back to her parents. "I'm not stupid, you know. I really do have a brain, though sometimes it seems that people around here don't like to give me credit for it."

"Now, Cyd," Rob began, but she silenced him with a glare.

"As I said, I'm not stupid. You get rid of the Lennons and old Wallace, you cut down on the parties, on the food, on . . ." She waved her arms wide. "On everything! At first I thought you didn't offer to help me buy the store because you wanted me to work on my own. Wrong, right? You didn't have the money, right? And all those jewels you kept saying were missing . . . I'll bet you a hundred dollars you were selling them in the city. Am I right again?"

No one said anything. They only stared blankly, and she hugged herself suddenly as though she were chilled.

Barton cleared his throat. "Robert, please call Abe and tell him what we've found here. Evan, call the office and tell them we won't be in today. For obvious reasons. And Cynthia—" she looked up and saw him smiling—"I think you'd better get your tail into work before you're late and Iris fires you."

The tension passed then and, after watching Rob dial the police number, she kissed her mother's cheek and ran out of the house.

Insane, she thought as she drove into the village. I swear they're all going to need keepers before very long. My God, how stupid can you get, not wanting to call the police? Melancholy swept over her almost as soon as the thought was done; an almost wrenching sadness that in her anger and frustration she had forced them to be truthful to her for once in their lives.

The money was going, going faster than they could make it; and on top of it a robbery to take the last of . . . what would she call it? Their legacy? Their stake?

Nevertheless, she reveled in a swell of pride at the ranks that had closed during the crisis, knowing that right at this moment her mother would be primping for the news photographers Marc Clayton was sure to send around from his paper, while Evan wrote a quick statement to be handed to the reporters. A laugh then as she parked in front of the store, louder when she saw Iris and Paul impatiently waiting.

"Boy," she said as she unlocked the door, "have I got news for you guys today."

And half an hour later Abe Stockton walked in.

"Hey," Cyd said from behind the counter, "you come for my statement or whatever you do?"

Abe Stockton could have been Paul's twin for the lines and the wattles, the New England stern that stamped his expression. He was wearing an ill-fitting dark suit and an out-of-fashion thin tie, his white shirt bunching at his waist when he opened his jacket to hitch at his trousers. He wore no overcoat though the day was chilled, a trademark he tried to foster until January brought the real season.

"Hey, Abe, you hear me?"

Stockton frowned and scratched at his head, the wisps of faintly red hair that clustered about his ears. "Statement? I came in here to see how you're doing, maybe pick up one of them new cop books you got there in the window. Then I got to go over to the bank to see about a loan. Why do you think I'm dressed like a damned fool instead of a chief? Statement? What do I want a statement for? You bash your brother or what?"

Cyd almost told him, then grinned stupidly and tried to pass her question off as a joke as she showed him around, only half-listening to his comments both sour and complimentary. And when he had gone, she called Ed from the back office.

"Listen," she said when Iris took the hint of her look and wandered out toward her husband, "you'd better get over here as soon as you're done work."

She paused, heard no comment, and said as softly as she could, "Ed, please say you'll come. I think I'm getting frightened."

# NINE

After sunset, paradoxically, the temperature rose to an unseasonable warmth and December seemed May despite the signs of Christmas. Low banks of fog billowed over the road partially obscuring it, freeing it as though a curtain had been raised, obscuring it again in a disturbing dead white that reflected the headlights back into her eyes. Cyd squinted, clicked the beams to low and slowed the car to a crawl a full hundred yards before she reached the entrance to the drive. Behind her she heard Ed's car grind loudly to a lower gear and she winced, yet she did not want to move any faster. Not because she might hit something or run off the Pike during those disconcertingly brief moments of temporary blindness, but because she was beginning to feel somewhat foolish about her panic-driven call. Fear was something she equated with a fast car on a sharp mountain curve in the middle of a storm, or leaning over a hundred-foot drop with little more protection than a flimsy wooden railing. This sensation was something new, something unusual. It had, for one thing, a direct connection with the confusion she had been experiencing since Thanksgiving, the unsettling notion there was something wrong with her world and she was helpless to define it.

It was, she thought, rather like being on a lonely road in an ancient automobile. The motor sounds right, there's no extraneous play in the wheel, yet one senses there is something out of place in the driving and tenses . . . waiting for the tire to go flat, the engine to miss, the electrical system to suddenly flare and burn out.

Tension.

She nodded to herself as she swung into the drive. That's what it was. That was what kept her from really enjoying the alien world of her bookshop, the Lennons' wry company, even Ed's hovering protection. A tension created by an entity she had always felt reasonably secure with, always at home with . . . her family.

The fog spattered in a light spray against the windshield, vanished beyond the reach of the headlights. Twice she thought she saw the quick red eyes of a deer far back in the shrubs and had jerked her head around to find it, could not, and shivered despite her buttoned-to-the-neck coat and the heavy scarf she had wrapped loosely around her throat. A trailing bough drummed on the roof. A stone thumped beneath the left front tire. She began whistling impatiently, tuneless, almost decided to call a halt to this nonsense and blare her horn when she reached the oval to let the others know she had arrived home safely.

Almost.

Not quite.

Instead, she cut the engine before leaving the drive and coasted with a light tire-hiss to the garage door and sat there, waiting for Ed to pull up behind her. Then she slipped out of her seat and waited for him by the trunk, her hands deep in her pockets, her eyes unable to stray from the black monolith she kept telling herself was her home. There were no lights on despite the hour, no way of knowing there was fog in the air except for the moisture that crept upon her face like strands of damp webbing. Somewhere in the darkness water dripped into a puddle, a tinny sound that should have been delicate.

When Ed touched her arm she almost screamed.

"Luck," he whispered with a nod toward the house.

She did not answer. Could not because she wasn't all that sure herself. At his urging then she led him around the side to the veranda, twice stumbling over protruding rocks in the grass, at the corner of the low wall barking her shin when she made the turn too soon. She cursed, rubbed at her leg, and stopped when they reached the library door. It was then that he snapped on his pencil flashlight, and she turned away quickly to keep from being momentarily blinded.

He grunted.

She looked up at the house and felt a light stab of regret. Less than two weeks before the holidays and there were no electric candles in the windows, no wreath on the front door, the usual display of colored lights gone from the tall fir in the center of the drive's oval garden. That, she remembered with a guilty stir, had been Wallace McLeod's job . . . and Sandy usually helped him.

"All right," Ed said brusquely, "let's get inside. I'm done here for the time being."

When he had met her at the shop after closing, the idea had seemed simple enough: instead of forcing a confrontation with her parents and brothers over the police, they would check first themselves on the nature of the burglary. It did not take much convincing for her to believe that she would receive no satisfactory answers from anyone if she faced them with the lie of contacting Stockton. What had shaken her, what had allowed Ed to maneuver her without much protest, was the inevitable conclusion that her near screaming attack on them that morning had only uncovered a surface conspiracy. There was money involved, to be sure, but evidently it was not the insurance payments they were after or they would not have hesitated to bring in the police. There were more lies beneath the lies, caverns of shadows she needed to be lighted before she could understand, and in understanding, confront.

"No lights," Ed said when her hand automatically reached for the switch.

"For heaven's sake," she snapped, "it's my house, isn't it?" But she dropped her hand and followed his dark outline behind the flashlight into the library where he moved immediately to the french doors and bent close to the latch. Then he turned slowly, aiming the thin beam at the stern-faced portrait. He shook his head.

"Idiots," he muttered as he crossed the room. "Looking behind a thing like that is the first place any pro would head for." He reached up with one hand and tugged at the broad, gilt frame, shifting it on its hinges to expose the face of the safe. He shook his head again. "You'd be surprised how many fools think something like this is safer than a bank. I would have thought your folks would have known better."

His left hand, encased in a snug brown glove, toyed with the dial for a moment, slapped at it once before he turned around

and flashed the light around the room, at the vases dearly
gleaned from private auctions, the brass and bronze figurines,
the leather, and the skillfully, expensively preserved books on
the highest shelves.

"There's a lot of money in here," she said, her arms folded and
resting on the high back of a chair. "What you're saying is,
someone knew about the jewelry and didn't waste any time with
all this stuff, even though it would probably bring nearly as
much."

"No," he said. He picked up a small brass horse from a square
onyx coffee table, brought it to her and held it up to the flash.
"Look at it," he said. She stared at him, shrugged, took the
boldly fashioned animal and gaped. Blinked. Wondered where
the weight was. "What I'm saying is, the thief knew that most of
this stuff was for show only. I would guess nine out of ten pieces
are worthless. And the way prices are these days, probably less
than that."

She took the flashlight from his hand without speaking, moved
numbly around the room and examined all those things she had
helped her father purchase. There were only one or two pieces
that were still genuine; the rest were forgeries, and not very
adept ones at that. Those who were around them every day
would not notice because they would not be looking for a
change, and so they would not see one; those who understood
the values involved, those from the outside, wouldn't grasp the
switch because they wouldn't have an opportunity for careful examination. But now that she could follow Ed's drift, she could
see it all, and in seeing ignored his warning and hit a wall switch
that turned on all but two of the lamps.

"It's a fake," she said, not knowing whether to cry or explode.
She looked at him for an explanation, but he seemed suddenly
weary. His shoulders sagged under the worn Navy peacoat, and
his eyes retreated to hollows beneath his brow. "It's a fake," she
repeated dully, and tossed the horse onto a chair.

Finally Ed nodded, unbuttoning his coat and dropping onto
the sofa. "So was the robbery."

"I don't think I want to know about it," she said, but sat anyway, retrieving the horse and holding it tightly in her lap.

"There's no outside lock on those doors. The glass hasn't been broken, the wood is still solid around the bolt. It fits closely. Any jimmying would show, the stain is too dark. Someone came into the room from the inside, took the jewels from the safe, opened the doors and left them that way. Assuming, then, that your family are the only ones who know the combination and it wasn't written down someplace . . ." He spread his hands wide, half in unnecessary explanation, half in sympathetic apology.

"I can't believe it," she said. "I mean, I know what it sounds like, but I just can't believe it."

"If they had called the police, Cyd, it would have been fraud. It's obvious. They did it themselves."

"I still can't believe it."

"I'm sorry, but I don't know what else to tell you."

She waited for the passing of several long breaths before rising slowly, dropping the horse to the floor and walking to the doors. Her hand touched at the curtains, gripped the latch and pulled it to her.

The night crept in.

Shaded lampglow slipped ahead of her onto the veranda, and the fog backed off quickly as though an animal wary of fire. Her coat was unbuttoned, her scarf unwound, but she stepped out of the room and walked toward the wall, trying not to think, not to multiply the implications from the first damned one. Yet she could see her way along only a single path in the maze—the morning confession of the selling of the jewels, the firing of the staff, artifacts replaced . . . there was no money. Or, considerably less than she had been left to believe. But where had it all gone that the Yarrows avoided official interference? Why had they sacrificed a sure payment from their insurance company simply to keep Stockton from knowing?

And something else, something more painful, and somehow more threatening: She had been cut off from her parents, from her brothers, as if she were little more than a side-effect not to be considered. If it were true that she was still loved, it was also true that they no longer trusted her. Without giving her a reason, she was not to be trusted.

Because of business? She wanted desperately to believe it, and could not. In spite of everything else they were a *family,* and she knew she would have been made even a small part of the fight to keep matters running.

Something else, then. Something that drained them, and would not let them talk.

*Whispering.*

She cocked her head slightly, a brief frown that vanished.

Rob and his solemnity was no doubt the most staunch in his belief that whatever was happening would not destroy the family; not even his father could best him in that.

*whispering . . . voices with words like dead leaves without wind . . .*

And Evan. Always the most nervous and therefore the most cautious. She could easily imagine him thrashing about in his bed every night, struggling for a clever way out of what he most likely thought was a one-way tunnel to abject poverty.

The idea came that perhaps they were being blackmailed.

*. . . the sound of a cat drifting across frost-stiff grass, a breeze across water, the moon behind clouds . . . whispering . . .*

Absently, she reached out a hand to touch the wall, and drew it back sharply. The stone was cold. Too cold. It almost had burned her. She looked at her palm, half-expecting a scar, saw instead trembling beads of moisture she wiped off on her coat.

Blackmail.

For a man in her father's position it would be easy. A youthful peccadillo come back in a haunting. Some not-quite-legal banking maneuvers. Her brothers, or one of them, involved with a woman, some indiscretion.

Blackmail.

She heard Ed cough behind her in the library, ignored him and was grateful he did not join her.

She wondered if there was a connection, then, between what was devouring the Yarrows and Doctor Calvin Kraylin. He seemed to have moved into a position of confidant long held, and rightly, by Angus Stone. Yet the lawyer had said nothing to her at all during their months of negotiations for the shop, not even a hint that he was displeased, or worried, or opposed to Kraylin's influence. Assuming, she corrected herself hastily, the influence was as strong as she was tempted to believe. But that was too simple, too much a part of B-movies and potboilers, where sinister doctors in soiled lab coats crept around corners and locked the doors to their offices, rubbing their hands gleefully in pitiful Lorre imitations.

*. . . insistent . . . demanding . . . hovering like a carrion hunter without swooping because the wounds had not yet drained life from the body rapidly dwindling to a corpse . . . waiting . . . whispering . . . the fog stalking through the trees, crouching by the shrubs, sprinting across the back lawn to wait patiently behind the wall . . .*

*The fog.*

My God, she thought, what is it?

She brushed a hand over her face as she half-turned toward the house . . .

*the fog*

. . . and saw the lamps blurred and darkening beyond the white curtains.

*had turned black.*

A dampness spawned in corners of dungeons, shadows of walls, tunnels of worms, rose from the flagstone and snaked about her ankles, climbed her calves to cling to her thighs. She shuffled half a pace forward. A pressure settled on her chest and bent her back at the waist, slightly, gently, but nevertheless back. She tried to lift an arm, but only her shoulder moved; downward to her fingers there was only a dead weight.

A certainty then: If she dared to turn around, if she dared move her head to look back over her shoulder, the glaring dead eyes of the lurking Greybeast would pin her to the blackening fog as surely as knives piercing her skin. It would grumble softly at her, taunting, teasing, daring, winking at a slim possibility of escape with a slight inclination that would send her scurrying toward the door before it snarled into life.

And again: The *something* she had sensed in the house before had returned, or had never left, and she understood now why she had always dismissed it—the other times, however many there had been, she had only been on the periphery of its presence. But now, this time, it was directed right at her.

It wasn't the Greybeast.

It was—

A bright light flashed in her face.

She leapt back, one hand thrown up to protect her eyes, the other extended behind her to grope wildly for the wall. And through the gap in her fingers she saw something dark, something black, sweep past the spot where her head had been.

The light dropped to a pool on the library floor, and she heard someone running across the carpet.

She looked quickly to her left and up, ducked barely in time to avoid being struck. A nightbird. She saw the lightning glint of one eye, the stab of its beak, the reach of its talons before it vanished into the fog.

"Cyd!"

Still crouching, not quite kneeling at the base of the wall, she saw Ed framed in the library doors, saw him jabbing at the black with his flashlight, futilely, helplessly, until the bird sprang from his blind side and he reeled back inside. Quickly, then, she was on her feet and running, one hand up in a fist to punch at the air, the other reaching for Ed as he tripped over a footstool and tumbled onto his back.

The fog moved into the house, and the lights were gone.

Ed swore as her hand grabbed his and yanked him to his feet, swore again when the bird darted overhead and its talons took a piece of his temple with it.

"The hall," she shouted, pulled him behind her as she thrashed through the obstacles the furniture threw up before her.

The bird dove again.

She felt a tearing at her shoulder and pushed at it angrily, shoved Ed out of the room and slammed the door shut. Leaned against it, panting, perspiration in rivulets dripping from her chin. The scarf somehow wound back around her throat, choking until she yanked it off and tossed it aside.

A loud *thud* against the door, the sound of something dropping to the floor.

Ed switched on the hall lights in their sconces and stared at her, his chest swelling as he fought for the too-warm air, blood seeping along his cheek to gleam on his shoulder.

"Damn," he said.

And with the word Cyd realized that during the entire attack, from the moment the nightbird had appeared outside, not one sound had been uttered, not a cry had been voiced.

The *whispering* . . . stopped.

She knew that reaction would not be long in coming, fought to delay it by taking Ed's hand and pulling him into the kitchen where she sat him at the table without him protesting. Then she snatched a clean dish towel from one of the cabinet drawers and soaked it in cold water, wrung it out and began to sponge the blood from his face. He shrank away at the first touch, closed his eyes and endured as she swabbed his cheek clean, the hair and flesh around the gashes at his temple. They were less deep than the blood-letting made them appear, and for that she was grateful. She did not want to think of what she would have to do next. She did not want to think.

Moving, then, like a mechanical doll.

At the sink. Water. Red . . . pink . . . clear.

From a cabinet overhead—iodine, gauze pads, adhesive tape; her hands drifting through the air in exquisite slow motion, feeling nothing, touching nothing, disembodied as though under control of another.

Back at the table. Ed hissing when the antiseptic flowed redly into the wounds, fingers with another towel daubing at the streaks that stained his skin, applying the bandage somewhat clumsily though effectively enough.

Returning to the sink.

And . . . slumping, gripping hard the stainless steel rim while spasms of cold, of heat, of myriad shades of fear coursed along her arms, her spine, the backs of her legs. She shook her head when Ed called to her, lowered her face toward the faucet and splashed cold water to her eyes, her lips, until at last she was able to swallow without tasting bile.

Then she turned around and looked through the door to the library opposite.

"I have never been in a kitchen this size outside a restaurant," Ed said.

She blinked. "What?"

"I've never seen such a place outside a restaurant, I said. All these beams, things hanging from the walls, enough cabinets with food for an army . . ." He swept his hands over the table. "This thing alone is big enough to seat the whole town, you know."

Shock, she thought. She put her hands on the back of a chair and stared at him across the table. "I'm all right," she said.

He grinned. "Then you're a better man than I am, Gunga Din, because I feel like hell."

A drop of cool water dropped from her jaw to the back of her hand. "I said I was all right."

"M'Lady," he said, "believe me when I say that this is just as much for me as it is for you." He paused before looking to his right toward the hall. "What the hell was it?"

"I don't know. I thought it was a crow, something just as big."

"Straight out of Hitchcock," he said, shaking his head.

"DuMaurier," she said, unable to keep back a grin. "She wrote the story. He only made the movie."

"I stand corrected," he said, rising, waiting for her to join him before leaving the kitchen to stand in front of the library door. "When you closed the door, it hit it."

"I know. I heard it hit the floor right after."

They stared at the doorknob for several seconds before she began to laugh, turned around and leaned back against the wall. When he looked at her quizzically, she could only wave a hand until the moment passed; then swallowed and brushed a hand down the front of her blouse. "I'm sorry," she said, "but I was thinking of all those stupid movies where the heroine knows damned well there's something terrible on the other side of the door, and she opens it anyway because she hasn't got the brains to run the other way. But," and she reached out, took hold of the knob, "I've got to know. And if it's still in there, it can't surprise us anymore."

"Whatever you say," Ed said. He looked around him for something to grab, then motioned her to wait while he returned to the kitchen and brought back a chair, hefting it by his shoulder like an awkward club.

He nodded. Once. Sharply.

With one swift move she flung the door open and leapt back to the wall, Ed stiffening, his eyes automatically raised to the ceiling. But nothing attacked them, nothing flew out, and the black fog in the library was gone, the lamps burning softly as though the house were normal and December a comfort. Cyd edged into the room then, frowning as she searched the upper reaches of the bookshelves, the tops of the oils, for signs of a shadow, a movement . . . anything. Slowly, she sidestepped across the carpet toward the french doors, took one quick look outside before pulling them to and throwing the latch and the bolt.

Ed set the chair down at the threshold, moved to his left, looked down and stopped. "Here," he said quietly.

"Is it dead?"

"Come see for yourself."

"I really . . . just wrap it in something. I don't want to see it."

"You'd better," he insisted.

"Please. Ed, I've had enough."

"Cyd, if I tell you about this later, you're not going to believe it. You'd better come over here and see what I see. At least, I think I see it."

Intrigued, and revolted, she walked cautiously toward him, her eyes not wanting to lower their gaze, lowering it anyway until she saw the huge crow lying against the baseboard. From the angle of its neck she knew it was broken, looked immediately to the back of the door and saw a deep gouge where it had struck there head on; then she looked back down again, spun away to grip the arm of a chair.

"Impossible," she said.

"Sure it is. Impossible put this mess on my face and tore a hole in your coat."

Her hand jumped to her shoulder where she felt the ragged gap.

"But it couldn't be," she said without turning around. "Ed, it only has one wing."

# TEN

"I still say we should have kept it and brought it in to Abe."

"Oh sure, just like that. Say Abe, we have something to show you. Seems that we were attacked by a one-armed bird that tore a hunk from my friend's face here and ripped my coat to shreds. It crashed into a library door and killed itself. Sure. Just like that."

"Wing."

"What?"

"It's a wing, not an arm."

"For God's sake, Ed!"

"All right, all right, but I'd still like to know how it did that."

"So would I, believe me, but right now I have something else to do. I have to find out exactly what my father's up to, and since he's not talking, there's only one other person who can help. Then, Ed, we'll take care of that bird. But not before."

"You're saying it's connected."

"I'm saying that it's just after nine o'clock on a Thursday evening and I feel like I've been up for twenty-four hours straight and I'm tired and I'm sore and I'll be damned if I'll be stampeded into doing something stupid."

"Assuming this isn't stupid."

"One thing at a time, Ed. One piece at a time."

"You know, for someone who's just nearly been nailed by the impossible, you're acting awfully calm."

"Don't you believe that for a minute, Ed Grange. Don't you believe it for a minute."

They drove the Pike carefully, Cyd watching the road grey under the headlights and vanish, an endless stream of transformation that made her drowsy despite the fact that she continued to replay the scene at the house so often it was becoming mechanical, flat, devoid of the terror that had engulfed, then left her. She knew that Ed was right, that they should be doing something about the bird, learning how, why, a dozen other questions that fought for priority when she let go the reins. But she could not. Dared not.

You should leave, you know, a persistent thought nagged her. You're just like that heroine you laughed at before, opening the door when you know there're monsters on the other side.

Could not.

Dared not.

No matter that her family had shut her out, no matter they had excluded her from the struggle to survive—they were, after all, her family at the end. Vain, foolish, stubborn . . . whatever. They were her family, and she would not leave them.

Whether they wanted her or not, she would not leave them.

She was about to attempt an explanation for Ed when he grunted and turned a final corner, a block south and east of the Oxrun hospital, and she pointed quickly to a small, ranch-style home. It was set back from its neighbors and surrounded as far as she could tell by an evergreen hedging carelessly trimmed in vaguely circular shapes. The lawn was unkempt, the concrete walk to the front stoop cracked here and there. But comfortable rather than decrepit, she thought; her mother would have said it had that lived-in look. The house's appearance was certainly not for Angus Stone's lack of clients, or his fees. Had he wanted, he could easily have lived beyond the park himself; but she knew him well enough to understand that he placed great store in living with himself as well as having something solid to leave to his grandchildren, that something being a small, impressive fortune in well-invested bonds and real estate in other parts of the country.

When she knocked on the door there was no immediate response, though a light glowed softly behind the front window's white-backed drapes. Ed stood beside her, obviously feeling out of place, and she took his hand to squeeze it. When he grimaced she grinned, and the door suddenly opened.

Stone was startled, recovered not quite fast enough that she didn't miss the expression. He was portly, short, his hair reduced to a close-cropped halo of lingering brown. Where in youth his face had been round from cheek to nose to chin, now it was slowly falling in upon itself and creating hollows where none had existed before, crevices where wrinkles had been, accenting the too-wide eyes that glinted when he finally recognized her. And had it not been for the animation that sparked him, he could have been called ugly, perhaps even grotesque.

"My dear," he said with a glance to his wristwatch. "My dear Cynthia." He reached out to take her hand, paused in the movement when he saw Ed beside her. "Eddie! My goodness, a convention, my dear? Ah well, then it's obvious you haven't come by just to share a cuppa with me."

Cyd followed him inside, amazed as always at the incredible amount of furniture and bric-a-brac he had managed to cram into every inch of space, and she almost laughed aloud at the thought that he probably spent hours every day trying to arrange some marvelous way he could use the ceiling as well for his myriad collections. She took the nearest chair, a Boston rocker, and waited patiently while the lawyer pointed out to a bemused Ed the various displays of porcelain and china figurines that ranged from a hundred breeds of dogs to Thai temple dancers to the small fireplace mantel over which he had taped and tacked framed photographs of himself with dozens of Senators, a handful of Presidents, Station council members, and lifetime directors of the world's financial community.

And when finally they were settled—Ed in a Queen Anne brocaded in royal blue, Stone on the deacon's bench in front of the window—she opened her eyes and stared at him.

"The store's doing well, or so I hear," he said, a familiar tic marking a corner of his mouth.

"It's only been four days, Angus."

"A good sign nevertheless," he answered with a wave. "I hear talk, you know. People are impressed. You won't make a fortune, my dear, but you won't starve either." He turned quickly back to Ed, a slight frown on his face. "Did you two have a fight, or was it a door you ran into," he said, pointing at the patch.

Ed shrugged; the frown deepened.

"Angus," she said before Stone could press further, "you were speaking of fortunes." She kept her voice low; there was no need to force him.

"Yes," he said then, with a tired slow nod. "Yes, well, I was wondering when you'd come to me about that. Of course, I'd hoped things would work out differently. A pity. But I admit to being surprised, Eddie, that you've become involved."

"I wasn't, until tonight," he said. "Things just sort of . . . happened."

Stone waited for an explanation, looking from one to the other until he understood there was none forthcoming. He grinned weakly, pushed back on the bench and pulled from his tweed jacket pocket a meershaum that he placed between his lips and drew on dryly, left it hanging to talk around it.

"Oh come on, Angus," Cyd said impatiently. "They're not going to tell me, so you might as well. I guessed this morning about the jewels and things, and I know now about all the other stuff."

"What stuff?" he said.

"You know, the library, the things Father's sold."

"Ah yes. Of course." He began rubbing a thumb absently along the side of the pipe bowl. "You know, Cynthia, I'm not really sure I should be talking to you after all, since you've not spoken to your parents yet . . . at least, you've not had them tell you exactly what's going on. I don't think it's my place—"

"Your place," she said quickly, very nearly harshly, "is to protect the family, Angus, and give us advice when we need it. Well, I'm needing it, and I need it now! I'm being prevented from having information I must have."

"Why?"

"Why?" She looked to Ed, who was staring at his hands clasped in his lap. "Why? Because I'm family, Angus, that's why. What affects my brothers, my mother, my father, has to affect me. And this is certainly not something that's not going to reach me sooner or later."

Stone brushed at invisible ashes on his chest, tugged at an earlobe while he stared at her thoughtfully. "You're right, of course. At least, I think you are. I'm just not sure that your father wouldn't want to tell you himself."

"Angus, he had plenty of opportunities this morning, believe me. And like an idiot, I took his word for something and let it go, thinking I would get to him tonight. But he's not home. No one is."

"Well . . ."

"Angus, how bad is it?"

His expression was blank.

A clock chimed the half-hour on the mantel.

"Very bad," he said finally. "Very bad indeed. There are, of course, some things that not even I am privy to, but I think your father would not argue the point if I told you that he is very close to filing for bankruptcy."

"I don't believe it." A declaration of fact, not an expression of wonderment.

It was Ed who had spoken; Cyd was too stunned.

"Be that as it may," Stone said simply, "I expect him in my office any day now. Any day. From what I understand he cannot last much longer."

Cyd wiped a palm over her face, hard, slowly, hoping that some sparks of pain would clear her head of the roaring that filled it, and echoed. Then, a moment later, a glass of cold water was pressed into her hand and she took it, emptied it, touched at her lips with the back of a hand. She did not know who had given it to her, and did not care; she could only hear the lawyer's deliberately cultured voice droning through an explanation of what bankruptcy meant, what it would mean for the family's financial future.

"My biggest problem is," he concluded, "I don't know where most of the money has gone. Of course, taxes both local and national make it hard for what we call the 'small wealthy' to hang on once the bites get larger, and if there's no extensive background of money within the family there's a natural tendency on the part of creditors to shy away from such risk-involved loans as would be needed in this particular case.

"But that's not the main stumbling block. I've been trying for a year to break through your father's stubborn streak, Cynthia, and he simply is not being responsive. In fact, except for that day I gave your shop's papers to him and Robert, I have been virtually unable to communicate with him on any level at all."

He examined his hands closely then, returned to rubbing the bowl of his pipe. "To be frank, as I'm sure you'd want me to be, I've been thinking quite seriously about complete disassociation. I refuse to work in the dark. It's as simple as that."

They waited for her to say something; she could only set the rocker into motion and stare at the pictures arrayed over the fireplace. Feeling a warm and growing rage work round her heart until at last she demanded, loudly and hard, why she had not been told about any of this, why she had been kept in the dark, especially when she and the lawyer had worked so closely together over the purchase of the shop. And immediately she had done it, she regretted it. Stone's face softened, sagged, and his hands lay limply on his thighs. The Harvard genius, the courthouse scourge was gone, and in his place a fat old man with pretensions of power. She did not like what she saw, hated herself for prompting it, and when he spoke the answer was not something she had not deciphered already—he had been ordered to keep his peace, and in doing so had felt a well of betrayal. And that was why, she thought bitterly, he had not charged her for all the work he had done for her, all the advice he had given her during their sessions when doubts had clouded her initial enthusiasm. He had dispelled them all with a wave of optimism she should have known was too great for his usual demeanor.

But she had been blinded by her own dreams. And by a good deal more.

Ed had risen and was standing by the hearth. "What did you mean, you don't know where most of the money's gone?"

Stone looked to Cyd, who nodded an echo. "Just what I said. All I know is, he's liquidating everything he can in the shortest possible time. At a loss, I'm afraid, he'll not be able to sustain."

"Kraylin!" she said then. "Damnit, I should have known he was bleeding them. He's probably got them hooked into some idiot scheme for that clinic of his."

"You mean Calvin Kraylin?" Stone said.

"You know him?"

"He's not a quack, if that's what you're implying, Cynthia. He's quite well respected in medical circles, and I know from my own dealings with him that he has more money than he knows what to do with. He's not your man, my dear, if there's something illegal going on."

"Are you sure?"

He looked again to Ed with a slight comical shrug. "Just like her father, wouldn't you say?" He took the pipe from his mouth and tapped it absently on his knee. "Cynthia, you can see that I am rather overweight for a man my size. And that, as you well know, is being charitable to an extreme. While you were gone, not long after the first of the year, I had what Dr. Kraylin called a mild fluctuation. It's also what the hospital called it. But I was impressed by the young man's manner, and he's been treating me ever since."

"Angus," she said, "Angus, I didn't know."

"No one did, until now."

She held a long breath, let it out slowly. "Angus, what am I going to do?"

"Be patient," he said softly, rising and standing in front of her. "Be patient. These are hard days for your father, and he's not used to them. Through a series of misadventures, plus using some simple arithmetic, you've learned what he never wanted you to know. At least, not until he was ready to give you answers as well as problems. Be patient. Be patient. In the meantime, I too will do what I can to . . ." He sighed, turned and walked slowly toward the door. "I'm tired, my dear. But I'm certainly glad I'm not alone anymore."

Once back in the car, Ed asked her where she wanted to go. She shook her head, waved her hands in an anywhere gesture.

The fog had thickened. Streetlamps blurred like moons behind cloud wisps. Shadows lost their edges. The few cars they passed were moving at a crawl as though there were no light at all to show them the way. And despite the warm night it was cold in the car, and she hugged herself tightly until her arms began to ache.

"Why didn't you tell him about the bird?"

"I don't know."

"Well, you can't be mad at the old man, can you? He only told you what you'd guessed already."

"I know that, I know that. I know exactly what he told me."
And I wish, she thought, I knew what he hadn't said.

She stared out the side window, at the black, at the grey, at a
world that was keeping her more than just figuratively in the
dark. Her left hand moved to touch her right shoulder, and her
fingers toyed with the gap in the cloth.

"Is it all that bad?" he asked gently. "I mean, losing the
money, is it all that bad?"

"It . . . it isn't the money," she said, "not the money at all. I'm
not so stupid that I won't miss having it around to get what I
want when I want it. But that isn't the problem. I mean, I have
the store, Ed. I know it's hard to believe, but that's worth more
to me now than anything behind those fool walls on the Pike.
For the first time since I don't know when it gives me a sense of
. . . it makes me feel as if I belong someplace. I haven't felt that
way about anything, not for a long time."

Ed shifted uneasily. "I didn't mean to pry, Cyd."

"You're not; believe me you're not." She smiled at her lap.
"You know, ever since I came back from Europe, I've been wandering around here feeling sorry for myself and soul-searching
and all that stuff people go through now and then. But for me it
was the first time. It's . . ." She frowned her concentration, sensing this was far too important to keep silent about. "Well, now I
know how Iris and Paul felt when they were let go. I mean, they
worked for the family and all, but they belonged there. It was as
much their home as their place now out on Hartwell. I never really felt I belonged on the Pike, not really. It was a place to go,
but it was never really . . ."

She could not say the word.

"But now I do belong somewhere. The shop. And it needs me,
damnit. It needs me."

Another block of silence as they passed in turn the hospital,
the Chancellor Inn, the high school, the police station. They
slowed in front of the park gates to watch a group of boys trying
to scale them, spot the car and scatter in a flurry of
whispers. Then they turned east onto the Pike, but as Ed moved
to swing into the Yarrow drive she touched at his arm and shook
her head.

He cleared his throat.

"What you're trying to tell me, then, is that I should stop trying to propose, that right?"

It hadn't been until he said it.

"Ed—"

"It's all right." He laughed. "No, it isn't all right, but that's the way it has to be. For now. You've got other things on your mind, like your family."

Her gaze lifted by inches from her lap to the dashboard to the streaks of grey light that speared into the fog. The windshield wipers thumped like twin metronomes. Her stomach became chilled, and the chill rose to her chest, her arms, and faded.

"I don't know them anymore."

"I know what you mean."

"No, you don't. I know what you're thinking, Ed, but that's not what I meant. I don't know them because . . . it's not them, Ed, it's not them." She felt hysteria forcing its way through the gaps in her words, swallowed hard to keep it down.

"You're not making sense, Cyd."

She felt the car slowing. "No, keep going."

"Look, I think—"

She waved him silent brusquely, saw him scowl then agree, and she wished she could be more precise, be able to tell him exactly what it was that had crossed her mind. But she was not sure herself. The idea that her parents weren't her parents, that even her brothers had somehow been substituted in her absence, was too farfetched to be granted credibility. Yet once said the notion stuck.

Physically, everything was the same. The mannerisms were there, and all those other things about them she knew more instinctively than intellectually. Yet . . . they were not the same people she had left at the airport when she had flown off to England. She did not know them, and she was sure now it was not because of the time not spent with them. It was not because she herself had changed all that much—though that too, she admitted, must be a part of it.

No, it was something else.

She straightened quickly.

The shop.

From the moment she had conceived the idea of Yarrow's and

had written to Angus about it, the shop had been more than just the beginning of a purpose she had not had before. It had become a barrier, an obstacle . . . she shook her head sharply. No. More like a thoroughbred's blinders that forced vision in only a single direction, and in forcing vision, forcing thinking.

Everything that had happened, from the first appearance of the Greybeast to the attack by the bird, had been too easily shunted to one side because she had convinced herself she had more important things to worry about at the moment, that the rest would fall into place when the time was right.

But there was no right time.

There was only now.

And with a wrench that was nearly a physical agony, she shoved the store aside. It would endure; it would be there when she was done.

Done, she thought.

Done with what?

Ed grunted.

She glanced to her left and saw a sudden flare of headlights at the side of the road, a car slowly moving out of the trees and falling in behind them. It was too dark to see the make or model, the color or the driver, but she twisted around in her seat and stared out the rear window.

"Ed," she said flatly. "Ed, it's him."

# ELEVEN

Greybeast, following.

She heard the creak of the accelerator, felt the car hesitate and thought for a moment it would stall. Ed swore softly, incoherently, and abruptly they surged forward, pushing her into the backrest. She turned back around, one leg drawn beneath her on the seat, one hand out to brace herself against the dash. There was no time to breathe; the air had turned arctic.

The fog turned to cloud that writhed past them in patches, clearing the road for yards at a stretch, suddenly closing them off to nothing but the sound of the engine, and the headlights maintaining a distance between them. Within minutes they had thudded over the railroad tracks, gates and reflectors snapping in and out of focus, vanishing as if they were only an illusion. Her throat went dry. Something small, something dark, raced out from the shoulder and before she could call out a warning she heard sickening multiple bumps beneath the chassis, saw Ed wince and grip the wheel more tightly as he chanced a glance at the rearview mirror.

"I should have a tank," he muttered.

She had no words to make him feel better, nothing light, nothing witty, only a weak animal sound that sounded like agreement as she stared at the headlights blaring behind them, desperately trying to pierce the glare in some telepathic manner in order to identify the driver, and by that the reason for his pursuit. She raised her free hand to shade her eyes, lowered it as soon as she realized the Greybeast was drawing nearer.

"Ed—" but he had already noticed, and the car eased forward again.

"Too dark," he said.

The trees had fallen away, and the shoulder was bordered by

low white posts strung with thick steel cables; amber eyes winked at them in passing, turned red as the posts grew taller and the cables became rusted rows of barbed wire. Beyond, through the dark and the cloudmist were deserted fields of small-parcel farms that had been cultivated in the valley since the seventeenth century, only recently succumbing to the malaise that had struck most of the rural communities throughout New England. There were a few that were too stubborn to yield, however, and every so often a long window light broke through the cover, seemingly static until it abruptly whipped to one side and was gone.

Was gone.

The car swerved sharply to avoid a pothole.

The limousine closed.

Who are you? Cyd demanded without making a sound, could not take her eyes from the diffusion of light that seemed to envelop them, sweep over the roof to join the headlights in front. A gaping seam in the road jarred her head around, and suddenly she remembered the last time she'd been out here.

"Ed, the intersection," she whispered, her knuckles pale on the dash.

Williamston Pike ended at a broad T-crossing, running into a two-lane road that bisected the valley north to south. Without turning around, however, there was no other way out—at either terminus the hills stalled it, chewed it, turned it into little more than a pair of trails that led, on the north, to deserted lumber camps, and, on the south, to a small iron mine that had long been played out before the turn of the century. She knew, then, their only chance was to take the right-hand turn at the crossing and reach the mouth of Chancellor Avenue, head back into the village before they were—

An exclamation escaped her before she could stifle it.

The Greybeast had drifted into the left lane, heedless of whatever traffic might be heading toward it, trying to pull parallel to Ed's smaller car. Gaining, only slightly. And with the harsh light temporarily bled from the interior she stared on ahead, trying to judge the time they had left before they had to make the turn . . . or smash through whatever barrier was set in front of them, into the field that lay beyond.

The headlights moved to a line with the rear bumper.

Ed was hunched over the wheel, perspiration falling from his hair into his eyes. He shook his head vigorously, and Cyd quickly wiped a palm over his brow. And felt the cold skin drawn damp and tight.

"Any time now," she said fearfully.

"I know, I know."

They pulled ahead slightly as the engine began a knocking protest that made her chest leaden, made her wish they were in her car instead. She glanced at the speedometer and wished she hadn't, looked up just as the fog tore apart in rags and she could see the stop sign slightly canted and glaring. Immediately, she braced herself as Ed applied the brakes, worked his hands to the left and, at the last possible moment, wrenched the wheel around to the song of screaming tires. She nearly slid into his lap then as the car fishtailed on the damp road, thudded onto the opposite shoulder and tightroped for nearly fifty yards before sliding back to the tarmac.

An oak tree reached out, scraped and missed them.

Another pothole bounced them so hard she nearly struck the ceiling.

And when she finally looked behind them, the limousine was gone.

She closed her eyes. Opened them. Let her hands fall into her lap where they fluttered weakly toward each other, clasped and were still. And there was no sound beyond the wipers and the tires and the increasing sharp agony of the overheated motor.

No explosion. No crash.

Ed slowed, made the turn onto Chancellor at virtually a crawl.

As he passed the railroad station, dark and hulking save for the red-and-green warning lights that flanked the tracks, he sighed and pulled over. Set the handbrake. Lowered his head until his brow rested on the steering wheel. He took several deep breaths, shuddering violently until Cyd broke through her stupor and lay an arm around his shoulders.

"How did he know?" she said to the windshield. "How did he know it was us?"

"Maybe he didn't."

"You don't believe that for a moment, do you? Any more than

you still think the last time was just a bunch of kids out for a ride. I know you don't believe it. Not now, anyway."

"No. But I'll tell you the truth—I wish to hell I did."

She sat back, slumped, rested her head on the back of the seat and stared blindly at the roof. She felt as if she had run four hundred miles, four hundred miles without respite or water; and wondered for a moment what kind of animal they had hit. She tried to remember if groundhogs came out after sunset. Unless it was a rabbit. A fox. She wondered if it mattered.

Ed tried a dry whistle. "I don't like to say this, Cyd, I don't want you to take it the wrong way . . . but I really don't think you'll want to stay at your place tonight."

"Ed, come on! It wasn't one of my folks who was trying to kill me."

"But they weren't there before, and they may not be there now. And if you don't mind, I really don't feel like driving the Pike again tonight."

"Ed, look—"

"You look, Cyd—I've got a bed and a sofa. Make your choice soon because I'm not stopping until I get there."

The only thing she could do was sigh, and nod. Knowing that there was nothing in the world that would let her sleep; knowing too that unless she did, she would lose all control.

And when she awoke, the afternoon sun fell loosely into the small bedroom. She tried to rise, gasped at the ache that exploded inside her skull, and fell back onto the pillows, eyes closed, mouth open. Counting slowly to one hundred as she remembered Ed practically carrying her up the steps and into the apartment, undressing her and forcing some kind of pills into her throat. She had gagged, but she'd swallowed, and as he sat on the mattress holding tight to her hand she had felt herself sailing, gliding, then falling into black.

There were no dreams.

Or none she could remember.

A shuffling, and she tensed, her hands gripping the bedclothes and pulling them to her chin. Waiting. Listening. Until an out-of-tune humming made her smile, relax, let her stretch her arms over her head.

"For a minute I thought I had given you too many."

She grinned more broadly, saw him standing by a battered dresser with his overcoat on.

"How do you feel?"

"If I said I felt wanton, you'd make some crack about soup, and then I would have to say something about your being in duck soup for ages, and then you would say something about Groucho, and then I'll demand to know if that's a crack about my disposition, and then you'll have to—hey!" She laughed and squirmed from beneath the covers when he tossed a hair brush at her and bounced it off the headboard.

"Your clothes are in the front room," he said.

She walked past him quickly, tensing for a pinch or a slap, at the same time pleased and disappointed he did neither. Then she saw the alarm clock set on an endtable. "My God, Ed, it's quarter to one!"

"I called Iris first thing and told her you might not be in today. I made up some story about celebrating last night. I don't think she approved."

"Would you if you were Iris?"

He moved to a ladder-back chair that sat near the door and leaned back to watch her. Arms folded. One ankle over the other. "I . . . I was wondering what you're going to do about last night."

"I never touched you."

"I didn't mean that."

She sighed as she sat on the lumpy divan and pulled on her shoes. "I know that," she said. "And I don't know. My God, my head hurts!"

"The pills. It'll wear off once you get some coffee in you."

"Great. Wonderful."

"Meanwhile, I thought I would do some prowling around, see if I can't come up with that damned car. Or maybe somebody who knows it."

"The police?"

He shrugged. Then reached for the door. "Cyd . . . you know, I'm sorry I didn't believe you the last time."

She nodded and gave him a shrug in return. And when the door closed, she stared at it for several minutes before rising and finding her way to his kitchen, grimacing at the remains of his last several meals, poking and searching until she had found the instant coffee and keeping her mind a blank until the kettle was boiling to a high-pitched whistle. Then she carried her cup to the window, stared out and down at the face of her shop. A customer walked in, several walked out, and she wondered why she wasn't happy because they carried large bags.

The shops, the cars, the people seemed so . . . small. She realized then that she'd never seen Centre Street from a height before, and the perspective it gave her was a curious one, as if she were staring into the open roof of some little girl's doll house, with wind-up vehicles and wind-up people and a small fan at one end to create a false breeze.

It didn't seem real.

Last night wasn't real.

Nor was the first time, and neither was the fire.

"Wrong," she whispered, set the cup on the sill and hurried into the bathroom where she ran a comb through her hair and fought back the melancholy when she saw the lines by her eyes.

Ten minutes later she was down in the shop, grinning at Paul's sly jibes about hangovers and parties, chatting quickly with several people who wanted to greet her, then moving into the back where she called a cab to meet her as soon as it could while she explained to Iris that she had simply a million things to do and she would be taking most of the afternoon off, would it be too much to ask if someone would help Sandy with his first day when he came in at four, he would be staying until nine, but don't wait for me if I'm not back at five, unless one of you thinks that Sandy couldn't be left alone.

Iris tried not to laugh, tried not to frown, and Cyd shook her head slowly and kissed the old woman soundly.

"Iris, I know you think I'm nuts, but bear with me, all right?"

"So what else is new?" Iris said, and looked back to her ledgers.

The taxi left her at the foot of the drive.

Sometime past midnight there had been a hard rain, and islands of mud and dead leaves dotted the blacktop, broken twigs in profusion and a long string of pebbles where the water ran off from the house to the Pike. The sky through the trees was a sharp winter blue, and in spite of the return to a near-freezing temperature, she left her coat open and her hands from her pockets. Her purse thumped against her hip as she walked. A cardinal on a limb overhead eyed her without moving. There's nothing sinister here at all, she told herself as the house came into view; it's just the way it always is, isn't it, my girl?

A bird called, and she jumped, brushed a finger through her hair and ordered herself calm.

And when she was able to move again, she knew there was no panic. Not now. Not again. Now . . . there was anger in the wake of her fear; and a rage she knew would be useful as long as she kept it channeled safely about the walls of her reason. A rage born of a notion she had had in the cab: that Angus had been trying to protect her by not telling her a thing, that her father and brothers were doing the same, and Ed in his gentle way was playing the Knight too hard to her Lady. Protection. As if power to act were something she lacked behind her carefully wrought facade of individual strength. As if they all believed they could see through her, through a world-weary, wealth-weary, age-weary shell of gleaming lacquer to an interior composed of nothing but fluff of the stuff dandelions are made of that scatters in a high wind to cower in the shadows, take root and produce only more of the same.

At the foot of the oval she paused to stare at the house. On the day after Thanksgiving she had thought the place smaller by virtue of her growing older; now it was smaller still, huddling beneath the abrupt keels of white-and-grey clouds that sailed overhead before an unfelt wind. The sky was still blue, but it was beginning to haze, and she judged that before sunset the blue would be pale. She glanced to her right—all the cars but her own were gone from the garage. Again her family was gone, to somewhere she was sure was not the city, and she felt more than foolish for not noting it sooner—that more often than not she'd been in the house alone.

For a change she was pleased; it would give her more freedom.

To do what, she asked herself as she let herself in. From the moment she had left Ed Grange's apartment she had been acting as if she thought she knew what she was doing, behaving as though she knew what she wanted. She unbuttoned her coat as she headed immediately upstairs. To do what? An admittance, then, that she had no idea. Except that if she searched, if she took the house one step at a time, if she stopped trying to find handles to hang on her confusion then she would more quickly find the key . . . any key at all . . . to any answer at all.

She began with her parents' rooms, then, unashamed and un-caring. Through desk drawers and bureaus, under cushions, be-hind curtains. For a time she felt silly at looking over her shoul-der when the house began creaking and the wind finally rose. But it was daylight, she told herself when she headed toward the back; in daylight there are shadows that are made by the sun.

Evan's rooms. Empty. As spartan and cold as the man who lived there. One picture on the bedroom wall facing the four-poster—a blurred photograph of her grandfather in uniform. Army. Major. She thought the term was: cashiered.

The more you know, the less you understand, she thought as she left for Rob's suite and stood on the threshold. Here the decor was as masculine as she thought any room could get with-out dead-eyed trophies staring down from the walls. The colors were dark, earthen and solid, as was the furniture placed in such a way that a minimum of paces would take him from studying to sleeping, from sleeping to leaving. It was an old man's room, and it began to make her nervous.

Daylight, she reminded herself sternly. There are no ghosts.

And there was nothing in any of the drawers she could open; no papers, no books, no deep secret diaries.

Foolish.

She felt a warmth around her throat as a blush began to form, and she almost walked out without checking the desk—a nine-teenth-century pine roll-top tucked carefully into the far corner of the parlor. Foolish again, but this time because of her hesita-tion; as long as she had invaded the privacy of the others, why should Rob be any different, then? She almost laughed as she crossed the room, a low nervous sound that belied the decep-tively warm sun that caught the colors of the carpeting and flashed them to the walls.

The drawers down the front yielded her nothing. Papers, nothing more, about the running of the bank, deals made and deals lost, an overwhelming amount of legalese that meant nothing to her. She closed them all softly, stepped back and pushed at the top. It was locked. She pushed again with the palms of both hands. Nothing in the house had been denied her until now, and she knew that her sudden impatience was unreasonable, and wrong. This was Rob's property; Rob was her brother; and it was quite well possible that he had a life of his own she had no business knowing. But the top was locked, and her rage was seething, and if she left this alone she might be missing one of the answers.

He can scream at me later, she decided as she looked around the room, saw a pair of crossed Confederate swords on the far wall and fetched one before she could change her mind. He can scream all he wants, but damnit they've lied to me!

Carefully, she worked the tip of the ceremonial saber between the top and the base, next to the bolt. The steel was thick, bending only reluctantly as she pressed down on the hilt, slowly moving the blade until the leverage was secure. Then she leaned her entire weight on the weapon, grunting, suddenly afraid that the wood would be stronger.

It wasn't.

The top gave with a loud tearing shriek, clattered back into its slot as Cyd stumbled away, the saber falling to the floor.

"Lord," she said, moved back to the desk and stared at the pigeon holes and tiny drawers set into the back. Her fingers trembled; she ordered them to stop. Was careful to replace each letter, each card right where she found it, working so slowly that not even the light film of dust was disturbed. And despite her anxiousness to find some sort of clue—not knowing what it would be, but knowing she would recognize it when it appeared—she was relieved when she was almost done and had found precisely nothing.

Until the last drawer yielded a small sheet of pale yellow paper, folded in thirds. She shrugged and picked it up, was about to open it when she heard in the distance, outside the house, a faint grumbling sound.

A car.

She was sure of it.

Quickly, then, she jammed the paper into her pocket and closed the desk's top. Hurried into the hallway rubbing her arms nervously, stopping at the stairwell when she touched the rent at the shoulder. She grimaced. It was a reminder of something else she had planned to do, something a part of her had hoped she had forgotten. With a soft noise of disgust, she retreated to her own rooms and changed her coat, slipping into the camel's-hair warmth as she headed down the stairs. Stopped at the foot and listened. Heard nothing but the dreamlike whispering of the deep cellar furnace.

"Nerves," she muttered as she turned round toward the back.

The kitchen was empty, no signs at all that her people had been eating. In the sink lay the crumpled towel she had used to sponge Ed's wound, and she reached out to touch it, drew her hand back and rubbed it against her stomach. That, too, she was hoping she would not find. In not finding, she would have been convinced that the night in the library had only been a dream, a nightmare, a result of a forgotten drink at the Inn. And if that had been true then she would not have to go outside to the trash can at the corner of the house, lift the lid and take from it the bundle Ed had made from towels and the bird.

"You don't live right, old girl," she said with a half-smile.

Her throat scraped when she swallowed. She hesitated, then turned on the faucet and took down a glass from the shelf overhead. Filled it with cold water, sipped, gulped, scolded herself soundly for the beginnings of a cramp that roiled in her stomach. She shook her head slowly and reached for a brown paper bag, held it close to her side as she left by the back door.

The trash can was one of several aligned neatly along the outside of the veranda wall. She reached over and yanked off its dented top, closed her eyes and took a deep breath. The towel was banded in golds and reds, and she almost turned away from it, almost ran for her car. But its shape was innocuous, and she told herself firmly there was nothing inside that was harmful or deadly, nothing but the body of an impossible crow.

Gingerly, she scooped the bundle into the sack, rolled down the top and was about to turn the corner for the garage when she heard a car door slam.

"Damn," she said. Waited. Suddenly turned on her heel and went back into the house, down the long hall to the front where she stood at the front door. Fussing with her coat, her hair, she tucked the package under her arm and put a hand out to the knob.

The Greybeast.

As she heard footsteps moving slowly across the walk, she turned and stared helplessly at the living room, the sitting room, the stairs that would lead her to someplace to hide.

The Greybeast.

Before she realized what she had done, she had taken several steps back into the wide foyer and was casting lots for the direction she should take.

Then, "My God, Cyd, what the hell's the matter with you?"

The sound of her voice, and the scorn it carried, calmed her instantly. Resolve returned, and with it a sense of bravado that she knew was baseless except for her rage. If she opened the door now and found the Greybeast in the drive . . . but if she stood there like a frightened schoolgirl and it was only a neighbor . . . or Iris from the store . . . or Ed back from his checking . . . or monsters or vampires or werewolves or beasties—she laughed and flung the door open and stepped into the sun.

# TWELVE

The automobile parked in the drive was a relic; it was the only word she could think of that was appropriate, and properly insulting. Its color had once been a midnight green, but sun and winter had faded the shade to a patchy pale grey; stains of rust edged the wheel wells, crept up the passenger doors, stitched across the low, slightly humped roof. There had been an ornament on the hood at some time in its past, and too many years ago it had been removed, the gap in the metal unfilled and spreading. The chrome bumpers were dull, pitted, and as she moved slowly down the steps shaking her head in disbelief she could see that the rear one was wired to the chassis. She looked around the front lawn and saw no one, shaded her eyes against the glare of the intermittent sun and peered into the front seat where nothing lay but a cheap plaid cushion by the steering wheel, and a thick manila folder whose papers were dangerously close to spilling onto the floorboard.

Curiosity made her circle the car, searching for a nameplate, trying to remember if the bulbous hood and almost pointed grille was a mark of a 40s Pontiac or an early 50s Buick. Evan would know, she thought; his infatuation with such vehicles far older than himself was legendary among the Yarrows, though he had never been convinced that he should part with money for one.

The wind took the corner of the house in a sudden gust that trailed leaves behind it and shoved her lightly against the trunk. It was then that she remembered the bundle tucked at her side, and the nervousness returned. She called out, twice, began walking slowly toward the garage when a figure stepped out from the side of the house, waved and hurried toward her.

His overcoat was tan, and two sizes too big; his hat was an

outdated Alpine sport with a trace of a plastic feather still stuck in the headband. He took off one glove and extended his hand; Cyd took it without thinking, her smile automatic.

"I went to the store," Kraylin said, "and your woman there—"

"Mrs. Lennon."

"—said she didn't know where you'd gone. I took a chance on coming here, hoping I'd catch up with you." He peered at her closely. "Are you all right, Miss Yarrow?"

She took her hand back, unnerved by the cold of the flesh touching hers, trying to tell herself it was only the air and recalling vividly an identical impression she'd had in the house the first time they'd met. "I'm fine," she said. "Why do you ask?"

"Oh, the store and all, I suppose. I wouldn't think a new owner like you would want to be away from it for more than a minute."

Feeling inordinately foolish, and foolishly brave, she indicated the sack with a nod and a smile. "Things to do, Dr. Kraylin, things to do." Then she looked toward the house. "Is there anything I can help you with? I didn't hear you knock."

He slipped his glove back on and sidled past her to lean against the car. "I thought I heard something around back. It wasn't you, of course, because you're here, aren't you?"

"It looks that way, doesn't it?" she said, and stood solidly in front of him, feeling for all the world like a fifty-year-old matron protecting a brood of young girls in her charge. But though she noted the reaction with a hidden inner wince, she did not relax; there was something about the doctor that went deeper than his manner, was more than her adverse reaction to the beard-sans-mustache she thought made him look ridiculous. It was the attitude he carried about him on his shoulders, an attitude of such complete confidence in his control of events even outside his own living that she bridled. Retreated somewhat Olympian to her breeding of wealth. It made her sound like a snob, and for now she did not care.

"Well," he said, squinting at the house, at the grounds. "I've never seen the place during the day. It's really quite beautiful."

"It's been better," she said coldly. "When Wallace McLeod was here."

"Wallace?" Kraylin was surprised.

"You knew him?"

"Of course I did! My heavens, Miss Yarrow, he used to come out to the clinic now and then to tend to my gardens. Marvelous man, marvelous man."

"I didn't know that."

"Well, it wasn't for very long, I admit. He never said where he had worked before, so I couldn't have known he was with you people. But he was a genius with flowers and hedges, things like that. A shame he had to leave . . . what do they call it? Service? . . . it's a shame he had to leave you."

She only nodded. Sandy, she was sure, had never mentioned his grandfather finding another job. And how had the old man connected himself with the Clinic, of all places, when there were . . . she stopped the thought instantly, the answer more than obvious. Her mother, of course. Myrtle had felt guilty about having to let the old McLeod go and had probably prevailed upon the doctor to hire him parttime.

"A worse shame, of course," Kraylin said quietly, "that he had to pass on so young."

"He wasn't all that young," she said. "But you're right, he was young for his age, and he shouldn't have died." She turned away as soon as the last word reached home, wondering why she had made the statement come out in accusation. Kraylin, however, did not seem to notice; instead, he pushed off the car and began walking slowly toward the driver's side door. Cyd stopped him with a cough, gestured toward the house. "You haven't told me why you were looking for me, Doctor."

He ducked his head in embarrassment, swept off his hat and patted absently at his hair. "You know, one of these days I'll lose my head if I forget to screw it on in the morning." He laughed, a near-giggle, and replaced the hat. "It was such a beautiful day today that I asked your folks to come out to my place for a little . . . oh, what shall we call it . . . a little holiday, so to speak. I also wanted to have another look at your father, so I decided to combine some business with pleasure. Your mother suggested I try to find you and extend the invitation to you as well. Not," he added hastily, and just a little tardily, "that I wouldn't have done so anyway, but I'd thought that with the store you'd be too busy, if you see what I mean. That is . . . well . . ." He sniffed and began wiping a hand on the car roof briskly, a needless dusting to mark his error.

"Well, thanks," she said, suddenly feeling sorry for him, he seemed so pathetic in his attempt to climb out of the unintentional hole he'd dug for himself. But when he brightened, she shook her head. "But as you said before, Doctor, I'm afraid I'm just too busy with the store."

"A shame," he said.

She thought he actually meant it, and was angry at herself for thinking it could be otherwise.

"However," he continued as he opened the door and slid in, "you may be sure that you're welcome to my place any time you want. I'd be glad to show you around; if you're interested in that kind of thing, that is."

"Well, it can't be too dull," she said when he'd rolled down the window. "If you can get Evan and Rob out there to look at a mess of medical things, you must be doing something right."

"I suspect, Miss Yarrow, it's my game room they're interested in, not my facilities."

The tone was reproof, and her sympathy vanished. She stepped back when he switched on the ignition, then impulse made her lay a hand on his arm. "Dr. Kraylin, if it isn't too presumptuous of me—why are you driving around in this . . ."

"Heap?" he finished for her, a bare smile above his beard. When she nodded reluctantly, the smile became a grin. "Not all doctors are millionaires, Miss Yarrow. All the money I've made for the last ten years or so has been dumped back into developing my clinics."

"More than one?"

"Oh yes. I have a small one in Hartford's North End, another down in New York, and I'm working on creating still another up in Maine. A small place called Bridgton. I suspect you've never heard of it."

She shook her head, too ashamed for the moment to dare say a word.

"Nice people up there," he said, looking straight ahead. "A couple of them are a little strange . . . but that's something else, something I needn't bother you with." He reached down for the handbrake, released it and looked up. "Well, Miss Yarrow, I'm sorry you can't be with us this afternoon, and I'll pass on your regrets to your mother. However, should you have second thoughts, please be my guest for dinner, at least."

Before she could reply, he had pulled away and was driving slowly out of the oval and down the lane. Bewilderment kept her in place for several minutes, made her move thoughtfully toward the garage where she dumped her unpleasant bundle into the back seat of her car. She had planned on taking the dead bird down to the hospital where she hoped someone would be able to tell her whether or not the crow actually could have flown as it had, with only a single wing. Now, however, she wasn't sure if that's what she should do. In the first place, she thought as she backed the car out and headed for the Pike, she was only kidding herself if she really thought one of the staff would say sure, a bird can fly with only one wing, just takes a simple matter of guts and aerodynamics. Kidding herself to postpone the facing of a paradox. And in the second place, there was more lying swirling around her than she was able to take.

Her parents.

Her brothers.

And now . . . either Angus or Kraylin—the one said there was money, the other said there wasn't. And if it hadn't been for the spectacle of that run-down car, her first and natural inclination would have been to believe the lawyer.

Not sure.

Too many things . . . not sure.

Luckily, she found a parking space in front of the store, let her gaze dart swiftly to the window of Ed's apartment before hurrying inside.

There were no customers. Paul was sitting behind the counter with a book in his hand, his glasses propped on his forehead while he squinted at the type. He was too lost in his reading to see her pass by, and she grinned and wondered if she could walk out without paying; not on your life, she told herself as she headed back for the office—coming in is one thing, going out is another.

Iris was laboring over a special order form when Cyd rapped lightly on the doorframe to attract her attention. A bony hand instantly settled on the old woman's breast.

"Did I startle you, Iris?" she said, still grinning.

"No respect for the aged," Iris muttered, and pushed her chair back. "You coming in for the rest of the day?"

"I wish I could," she said, settling on a corner of the desk, shoving aside papers and ignoring Iris' frown. "But I still have some things to do. Listen, Iris, I need to know something—did Wallace ever work for the Kraylin Clinic after he left us?"

"Was fired."

"All right, all right . . . after he was fired."

Iris set a forefinger on her cheek and stroked the flesh lightly. Cyd knew she was stalling, that her memory was infallible even if her body was not. But she waited patiently, two decades of experience cautioning her that Iris Lennon was never ever to be pushed, not until she figured out what the information asked for was worth in her time.

"I don't know," she finally said. "Not really sure. He could have, I suppose. We didn't talk much after. He kept to himself a lot. Why?"

"Nothing, no reason. Just something I heard today."

"What's the Kraylin Clinic, anyway?"

She turned quickly. It was Paul with a question, the book he'd been reading still in one hand, a finger in the pages to mark his place. When he repeated his question, she told him what she was looking for, and he scratched at his temple with the book before sighing.

"Tell you the truth, I never heard of it. You, dear?"

"Can't say that I have," Iris said.

"For heaven's sake, Iris, why didn't you say so in the first place?"

"Didn't ask if I knew it," Iris said, as though the answer were too obvious to be spoken aloud. "Only wanted to know if Wallace did work there."

A voice from the front turned them all around, and Sandy McLeod—amazingly, handsomely dressed in a safari leisure suit —stood at the head of the center aisle with his hands on his hips. Cyd smiled broadly and hurried out to greet him, turned him around by the shoulders and demanded to know if he were trying to make them all look decrepit.

"Did I do something wrong?" he asked, suddenly unsure.

"No, of course not, Sandy, but this . . ." and she gestured to the suit. "My Lord, Mr. McLeod, you're going to make us all respectable if you don't look out."

The boy grinned, waved to the Lennons who had not followed Cyd out, then scurried behind the counter and began poking at the register. "Great," he said. "Man, I can't wait."

"Well, why don't you . . . I mean, you're awfully early, Sandy. Don't you think—"

"Early!" he said, pulling back a sleeve to stare at his watch. "Miss Yarrow, I just got this watch for my birthday. And according to this I'm ten minutes late."

Cyd was about to correct him, then looked out to the street and saw the shadows on the blacktop crawling swiftly toward her. There were lights glowing in the stores opposite Yarrow's, and the sun had already dropped below the roofs. Good Lord, she thought, how long was I out there?

"Sandy, listen," she said, quickly rebuttoning her coat, "I've got to run. Either Mr. or Mrs. Lennon will stay with you until closing. Don't forget to lock the back door and see to it that the deposits are put into the bank. Paul knows how much we should keep until tomorrow."

"But Miss Yarrow, this is only my first—"

"Please, Sandy, I haven't got time. Just be a good boy and do as you're told."

Sandy dropped hard on the stool as if he had been slapped, but Cyd was too suddenly caught up in an odd sense of urgency to stay and apologize and stroke the boy's ego. She stopped only once, the door opened and held by a cock of her hip, "Sandy, did your grandfather ever work for Dr. Kraylin, out on the Pike?"

"Who?"

"Never mind," she muttered, and raced for her car. Cut off a truck when she pulled away from the curb, cut off another when she turned a hard left onto High Street. A glance as she passed Ed's office told her it was closed. She frowned. Ten after four; unless he was still searching for the owner of that limo, he should have been there, or contacted her by now. A station wagon stalled at the next intersection made her want to lean on the horn, and her fingers drummed the steering wheel increasingly rapidly until at last the vehicle moved and she sped through the traffic.

The urgency grew, and she did not want to fight it.

It reminded her of a time when she had been nineteen and Rob had fallen from the wall behind their castle shack. She'd been at the high school that particular afternoon, talking with some of her old teachers about her first year at college. That same sense of *now!* had struck her almost physically, and she'd run several cars off the road in her haste to get home. And by the time she'd reached the lane, an ambulance was driving out—Rob had suffered a broken back and left leg, and only the intensity of care had put him on his feet again. Two years of struggling. Two years of therapy. A miracle, it had been said, that the spinal cord hadn't been severed.

For months she'd believed it had been a genuine, occult premonition, until it had been pointed out to her—by Angus, in fact, if she remembered things right—that she had known Rob would be fooling around in that area that day from something he had said to her only that morning; that she knew the condition of the wall, the weather, and the fact that he could never resist a tight-rope act when he was back there. Three years older and still playing the kid.

"Just a matter of putting things together," the lawyer had said. "It's happened to me in court, too. You stand there in front of the judge and suddenly, like someone whispering in your ear, a few of the loose ends aren't loose anymore. Disconcerting, to say the least; especially when the loose ends have a tendency to hang your client."

This time, however, there was no premonition, no portents of disaster—only a definite strong feeling that if she moved fast enough, hard enough, it would all come together. Like reaching for the ring on a carousel; one quick lunge and you have it, and the free ride is yours.

Fast enough.

Hard enough.

And when she saw Ed's car she almost screamed.

The Oxrun hospital took up the entire block facing King Street, between Devon and Northland—brick and grey marble, tall tinted windows on each of its two stories, a small parking lot behind and on either side. Over the four revolving front doors was an aluminum canopy that reflected the harsh red of the setting sun, and at the curb was Ed's automobile, its front end smashed in as though it had hit a pole.

Cyd braked instantly, felt the car skew before she regained control, and parked across the street in a space by a hydrant. There were only a few people about in the green and soft lobby, and she was able to calm herself before she reached the receptionist, ask about Ed without a tremor in her voice. And as soon as she had, a hand touched at her shoulder. She started, turned, saw Ed sheepishly grinning. There was a bandage wrapped around his brow, several stained cuts on his jaw and his neck. Blood stains on his coat. A small bandage on his left hand.

Not daring to speak, she took his hand and led him to a small waiting area where couches and chairs were hidden behind a proliferation of carefully tended plants, and an aquarium or two. When he sat, she stood in front of him, not knowing whether to be angry because he hadn't called, or concerned though there didn't seem to be any pain in his eyes.

"Well?" was the best she could do.

He shrugged. "I thought I saw him out on Mainland."

She waited. You idiot, she thought; you're a little old to play cowboy.

He swallowed and tried to brush at his coat. "I thought I saw him—as it turned out it wasn't him—so I took off after him. Somebody took a straight-away and turned it into a bend. The old buggy doesn't have it much these days. I wasn't going too fast when he got me—the tree, that is, so I guess I was lucky."

"Lucky?" She turned away and stared out the front window. Turned back with most of her temper in hand. "Lucky? You are crazy. You're crazy, that's all there is to it. Damnit, Ed, you're not a cop anymore, you know that don't you? You could have been killed!" The trembling began in her arms, traveled to her legs and she sat quickly beside him, grabbing his good hand and squeezing it tightly. "You're crazy."

"Well, maybe, maybe not. Right now I just ache."

She pointed toward the street. "How'd . . . you didn't drive that mess back here alone, did you?"

He shook his head, slowly. "No, some guy was there when it happened." He put a finger to the bandage. "It's just a deep cut, that's all. More blood than I thought I had in me. He, this guy, he wrapped a handkerchief or something around it and drove me straight back here. He knew some guys on the staff and they took care of me right away." He smiled, then, and postured. "Ain't nobody going to keep this fool down."

She tried to laugh, but the sight of his courage overlaying his pale face was too much; she looked away and wiped at her eyes with her sleeve. He was drugged, evidently, something mild to help the pain, and when she squeezed his hand again she was taken by the cold.

"Are you sure it wasn't him?" she said then.

"Pretty sure. Why?"

She took a deep breath and pulled all her thoughts together. "Never mind," she said. "I'm going to take you home and then I have to see Angus. There are a few things he told us last night that I want to clear up."

"Cyd, why don't you give it up?"

She looked at him harshly, her hand back to her lap.

"I'm worried about you," he said. "Why don't you just give your folks a chance—"

"How many times have I said you're crazy today? Well, here's another one—you're crazy, Ed. Everybody's talking to me and nobody's being straight with me. I can see a handful of generations of Yarrows slipping into the dust, and I'm not going to sit back and watch it happen without trying to contribute something."

"But you could get hurt." He jerked a thumb at his head, winced and dropped his arm.

"They didn't do that to you, Ed."

"Maybe not, but aren't you getting tired of all these coincidences? Cars chasing us to hell and gone through the valley, that . . . that thing at the house last night . . . why don't you just wait for your father to come clean, huh?"

She leaned back in the chair and stared at him, finding excuses for his behavior in the drugs he must have been given, the shock he must have had when he lost control of the car. But there was something more in the way he kept his eyes on her face, the way he sat so stiffly as if movement would make him scream. And when she knew what it was she almost could not face him—he was afraid, as much for himself as he was for her. Then, she thought, it had to have been the Greybeast he had been following, and it was the Greybeast, not his lack of skills or a sudden turn, that had driven him off the road. Ed Grange was afraid.

She had lost her rusty knight.

"I'll take you home," she said again. "Then I have to talk to Angus."

She rose, but he did not follow.

"If you don't mind, Cyd," he said after a long second, "I'm going to sit here for a bit." He smiled, weakly. "I don't think I want to be too far from a doctor just now. They took the X rays and stuff, but . . . I think I'd rather stay here. Just for a few minutes. Unless . . . unless you'll come in with me and sit for a while."

She could not understand what was happening to her, could not believe the words that she said, "I have to see Angus, Ed. I can't wait much longer."

"All right. That's all right. Come by later?"

His grin was infectious. She bent over and kissed his cheek gingerly, nearly flinched at the smell of blood and antiseptic, the cold she had noticed when she had held his hand. Then she walked back to the reception counter and waited for the nurse to finish on the phone.

"Miss," she said, with a nod of indication, "that man . . . he wants to stay here for a while. He was in an accident, a minor one, but he doesn't feel up to going home right now. Would it be all right . . . ?"

"Of course," the nurse said. "If you'll just give me his name, I'll be sure to let the doctor who treated him know. Just in case."

"Grange," Cyd said. "Edwin Grange. I don't know who brought him in, but I guess someone in Emergency will have all the details."

The nurse unclipped a pen from her breast pocket and noted the information on a pad by the phone, smiled, and Cyd walked slowly to the door. Ed had not moved. He was staring out the window, watching the air darken, barely breathing, scarcely blinking. There was a moment, then, when she wanted to go to him, to hold him in her arms and rock him until he slept . . . but it was only a moment, and she did not much like herself when she stepped out the door. Decided that since she was so close to Angus already, she might as well walk, to fill her lungs with fresh air.

A tow truck was hitching a chain to Ed's car as she passed, but she paid it no mind as she crossed King and headed down Northland. She tried, instead, to drive his image from her mind by rehearsing what she would say to Angus when she saw him. Determined that nothing would make her leave that house until she was satisfied that that quarter at least had yielded her all the information it had. And once that was done she would check on Ed, hoping she could make him understand, if he didn't already, that she hadn't deserted him though it seemed she was needed.

A windgust dropped her hair into her eyes.

A look to the streetlamps, another and they were on.

Her stride narrowed, her pace slowed, and in less than five minutes she was standing in front of the house. One hand lay lightly at the top of the hedging, and she scanned for a moment the homes on either side, and the street behind her. There was no sign of movement, no sign of life, just some cars in the driveways and red wagons on the walks and in the gutter near the corner a large green-and-white ball pushed at by the wind, trembling but not moving.

There was nothing at all massive about the lawyer's small ranch home, nothing she could see that was intimidating or foreboding; but she had a sudden impulse that almost made her race back to the hospital and hold Ed's cold hand, to warm it, bring life to it, to make him smile without the fear. Ironic, she thought with a broad border of acid—the Knight had been unhorsed and the Lady was riding. When an ambulance wailed she glanced quickly to her right, back toward King Street and its obvious destination. The impulse to return grew stronger, and she shuddered with it, fighting the guilt that spread black around her. Her ears began to sting, and she knew it was the cold; when her eyes began to water she whispered *it has to be the wind*.

It grew darker.

An old man in shirtsleeves came out onto the porch of the house next door, thumbs in suspenders as he watched her without malice. She brushed a finger beneath her eyes, looked once more back to King Street, then took a single step up the walk before she paused, and frowned.

The curtains in the front windows to the right of the stoop had fluttered, as though someone had parted them briefly and let go.

And she wondered how long Angus had been watching.

# THIRTEEN

After several spurts of knocking, each increasingly heavy, there was no answer. The doorknob would not turn; the porch light stayed dark. Several cars sped past with headlights too bright for comfort in the darkhaze dusk, and Cyd flinched as though the beams were lashes across her shoulders. She knocked again, as loudly as she could, barely resisted the temptation to call Angus' name. A step back to stare angrily at the windows to either side, accusingly at the door that refused to yield to her. Fists jammed into her coat pockets. A second search of the windows for signs of betrayal, and she hurried down the steps and across the front lawn. Shrubs packed the grass from the house to the hedge, and she threaded her way awkwardly through them until she reached the back. Paused. Waited. Looked sharply to her left at the nearest window as if expecting a face to be following her progress.

She scowled at the blank panes, at the curtains and shades behind them.

In the back the lawn was as ill-kept as its mirror in front, and the several apple trees that twisted close together were unpruned, and untended, their fruit in small piles rotting untouched on the ground. There were three low steps that led to an aluminum storm door, and she took them in a single angry bound that made her thrust out a hand to keep from colliding with the glass. Again she knocked, half-heartedly this time because she knew there'd be no one who would willingly admit her. She searched the frame quickly and found no bell, pulled the storm door open and tried the inner knob.

It gave.

She hesitated, not caring if anyone in the neighborhood saw her, only wondering if perhaps she were more foolhardy than brave. Someone had been watching her as she'd stood on the sidewalk—she was sure of it, she was positive; and as she tried to tell herself it was not her imagination a dozen alternatives flooded her mind until she fought them all back, and stepped inside.

The kitchen was small, immaculate, giving off a curious air of being unused. Everything was in its place, and everything was polished, and she felt it as sterile as a hospital room. Most likely, she thought as she stood by the small table, he dined out most nights, and when he was home forgot to eat.

She passed into the dining room, which was little more than the broad part of a stunted L-shape, the rest of which stretched across the front of the house to the door. A short hallway gave access to the bathroom and three bedrooms, one of which she imagined would have been his study.

She called out and waited, understanding her trespass and knowing that Angus would not call her on it if he were home. She was only a friend come back for a question, and if he were reading too intently or taking a shower or a nap, it was only quite natural that she should let herself in. After all, she thought, the Yarrows practically subsidize him, so it wasn't as if she were merely a client. And as she stood in the frame between front room and back, she realized how tense she had allowed herself to become, how her shoulders were beginning to ache across her back, and her nails were starting to dig into her palms.

"Angus! Angus, it's me, Cynthia!"

The name sounded strange as it left her lips, and she coughed loudly before trying it again, "Angus, it's Cyd Yarrow. I need to talk to you."

Well? she questioned silently; how long are you going to wait for an answer? The place isn't that big, you know. You going to stand here all night?

Slowly she stepped among the piles of journals and briefs, at the last minute deciding to walk down the hall. At the bathroom, then, she stopped and flicked on the light—to see nothing but her image in the large mirror over the sink. It startled her, but the light was comforting and she left it on as she headed for the last room on the right, sure this was his bedroom, and if he were here he would be napping.

The door had been closed to a finger's width crack, and she lay a palm to it and pushed. It protested. She pushed harder, and waited.

"Angus?" Softly.

A single bed was set flush into the far corner; on the wall opposite, a chest of drawers; on the floor between, a small braided rug of indeterminate color. Nothing else was in the room but shades on the two windows. The light from the bath gave the furniture vague shape, and something else on the bedspread, long and black.

"Angus?" Now fearfully.

She groped for a light switch and found none, and saw no table that would have held a lamp. She turned around, saw a white frosted dome on the hall ceiling and located the switch, flicked it up and looked back into the room.

Angus lay fully dressed as she had seen him the previous night. His shoes were on, and his tie carefully knotted; but there was a stillness in the air that disturbed her, and a dread lack of movement when she approached the bed and leaned one hand on the mattress.

"Angus," she whispered. "Angus, it's Cyd."

A passing truck flashed its lights through the window, illuminating the shade and added a soft white glow to the one from the hall. At that she stumbled backward, one hand out groping at the air to keep her balance. There was no sense calling him again; he was dead. The old man had, in the space of twenty-four hours, become ancient: his flesh sagged as if gravity had doubled, his eyes sunken into their sockets as though they had no support; his color was a pasty white just this side of grey, and his hair seemed perceptively longer, and unimaginably brittle.

A second flash from a second vehicle, and she could see Barton lying on his own bed beyond the park.

There was very little difference . . . except, Angus was dead.

She lurched toward the door, into the hall, kept a hand on the wall as she made her way to the living room where she collapsed with an anguished sigh into the rocker. The movement, gentle and steady, served to calm her until she was able to fight through the grief she was feeling. Angus Stone. Alone, old, confused by those he had thought were his friends. Angus Stone . . . dead . . . and she had no idea how old he was.

She licked at her lips several times before realizing her mouth and tongue were dry; scrubbed her hands together until she felt the skin burning. She rocked faster, harder, the chair a steed that would carry her away, through the valley and over the hills into what some called civilization, where sanity reigned and the lies that people mouthed were expected, thus compensated. And the faster she rocked the more she felt the wind of her creation, pulling at her face, disfiguring it, distorting it; faster to flee the implications of her grief.

She began to perspire. She ignored it.

She nearly slipped off the thin cushion, and pushed herself back.

It was that movement which broke the self-woven spell. The damp wood of the arms under her palms, the press of the wood into her spine—she snapped back to the room in which she was sitting, to the dogs and the dolls and the pictures and the hearth. The air was close, all the windows had been closed, and she opened her mouth widely to find a proper breath. Deeply. Slowly. As the chair slowed beneath her. Deeply. Softly. As the runners on the carpet wore into their grooves. She dipped into her coat pocket and pulled out a handkerchief, mopped her brow and her chin, her neck. Then she rose and crossed to the telephone that squatted blackly on an end table nearest the fireplace.

She called the police, the handkerchief wrapped loosely around the receiver. She explained what they would find if they came to Northland now, but she did not give her name when the sergeant on duty started fumbling with his forms. She hung up. Wiped her face again and hurried out the back door, stuffed her hands back into her pockets and walked as unconcernedly as she could to the sidewalk and the street.

She winced when a door slammed just a few houses down, but she did not turn around. She kept herself facing King Street, staring at the lights that blurred without fog until she reached the corner and saw her car. It was alone at the curb, and the entrance to the hospital seemed empty, seemed deserted. No visitors now; those who were coming were already inside, in the lounge or in the rooms, preparing themselves for their duty.

A slow and deep breath that nearly caused a fainting, and she got into her car and drove off toward the park. The steering wheel was cold, the windshield lightly fogged until she snapped on the blower; she felt as if she were in an alien machine, not the familiar steel friend that had brought her so much joy, had driven her into so much trouble—the green glow of the dash outlined her knuckles, made luminescent her coat, and as she turned the corner slowly onto Park Street she half-expected the moon to drift by as she settled into orbit.

Why? she asked herself. She was sure there must be a law she had broken in reporting Angus' death and not staying until the police arrived; and she was just as sure that by staying she would have defeated whatever purpose had been growing in her mind. To stay in that house—to stand in the living room while Angus lay dead on his bed—an image of his crumbling face floated beyond the windshield and she swerved sharply, bounced off the curb and found herself crossing the Pike, still heading north with the woods on her right and the Oxrun Memorial Park sweeping off to the left.

Why hadn't she stayed?

She felt no sense of danger, nothing like that at all. Not even the thought that someone had been watching her from the house before she'd entered bothered her now. It was only one more curiosity to add to the rest, and she had so many of them now that one more made no difference. Another grain of sand thrown onto the beach, another drop in the ocean—what difference did it make when she could make little sense of those things she had?

She reached out and punched the car lighter into its recess, waited, and when it snapped out pulled it free before she realized with a grin that she hadn't had a cigarette for at least a month. The need was there, but other matters overrode it. The orange glare of the coils faded as she watched them from the corner of her eye—like an ember drifting away from a fire, she thought; like—

Fire.

*And Miss Yarrow . . . next time please throw out all your*

*trash right away, okay? Stick it outside in back, in one of those
dumpsters or a metal container.*

When she and Ed had left the store after the firemen had left,
she locked the back door.

She shouldn't have had to; she had done it when she had left.
And the lamp was almost brand new—she had bought it in
Spain.

She pulled over to the side of the road, set the emergency
brake without switching off the engine. Warm air billowed from
the heater under the dashboard, but she rolled the window down
to let in the cold.

I *knew* it, she thought.

Fire. And the Greybeast—why had it stopped chasing her
when it had gotten so close?

Fire. And the Greybeast—if she were the target, then why had
it chased Ed? Why had it forced him off the road?

Because whoever was after her did not want her dead—that
much had been apparent since the very beginning. And whoever
was after her wanted her alone. Alone. With Ed gone now, his
spirit somehow broken by the stand-off with death, she had no
one but herself to fight her battles for her.

And it wasn't the store. She had had several ideas that there
were other merchants involved—jealousy, rivalry, some compli-
cated insurance fraud, something, anything, to keep her from
opening. But if that had been true, then the Lennons and Sandy
would not have been spared. Their work for her was not a secret,
they could have been reached at any time since that first day.

It wasn't the store.

It was her. Nothing more.

With a slap to the wheel she thought she'd found the purloined letter. Like the nose on her face it was right there in front
of her, seen only at angles, never recognized except in mirrors as
something that was whole.

She looked up and saw her face in the windshield: "You're a
fool, Cyd Yarrow."

The reflection nodded.

Snapping off the brake, then, she made a sharp U-turn and returned to the Pike, headed east past her home until she reached
the spot where she thought the Greybeast had been waiting.

Neither Iris nor Paul had ever heard of the Clinic.

*Sandy, did your grandfather ever work for Dr. Kraylin, out on the Pike?*

*Who?*

One in Hartford, New York, and Bridgton, Maine.

Her headlights were dim. She pulled off to the side and took the handkerchief from her pocket, climbed out and wiped the dirt from the thick glass. Back inside she waited until the night-cold had left her before easing out onto the road again, staring into the darkness on the left until she had reached the Pike's end.

There had been no sign, no paved drive, not one thing that she could see that proved the Clinic's existence.

She turned around and headed back, the car moving at just above a fast walk. With her left hand she held onto the wheel while her right supported her on the seat as she leaned close to the passenger door and stared out the window. Shaking her head slowly.

Lies built on lies.

She saw it.

Less than a hundred yards past where the fields ended and the hill-forest began there was a break in the tall brown weeds and thickets that served as a base for the wall of trees. The shoulder of the road was level here, without ditch or burrow to interrupt it, and it was graveled with small multi-colored stones to hide any tire tracks the Greybeast might have made. She pulled off to the side, as close to the shrubbery as she could, wincing as the winter-stripped branches scratched like iron against the paint. The headlights died. The green dashglow faded. And after the blower's whine had been cut off, the silence was too loud for her to take without shuddering.

Shop fire, bird flight, Greybeast racing.

She retreated back to her cinema world, found comfort there in scenes from films long gone, from titles long forgotten—she was dressed in white, edged in black, and the authorities had given her ten hours to leave town.

Get out of Oxrun, Cyd, before it's too late.

She sighed several times in melancholy rage—whoever among her family had thought she would run had not counted on her trip to make her restless, had not counted on the shop to give her an anchor. Perhaps he/she/they had thought she would fall madly in love with Ed Grange, and would prevail upon him to take her away from the Station and its madness; or she would drag him herself as she continued introspection.

Mother and her matchmaking, Father and his impatience, Evan trying to be so subtle it was like throwing flaming bricks. Only Rob of the four seemed to hold himself neutral, like an umpire seated above the arena where silent battles were waged, raged, flung dust into blindness. Only Rob knew his sister was something more than just a sibling, something more than just offspring.

Only Rob understood that his sister was alive.

All right, she told herself, so they were mistaken, okay? So they didn't count on the shop to act the way it did. So what? What good, my girl, is knowing that going to do you?

Reason then tried to convince her she should stay in the car, turn on the ignition again and drive into the Station. Park on Chancellor Avenue in front of the police station and sit on the desk sergeant until Abe Stockton was brought back to his office. While there she could call Ed to see if he were feeling better—he really should be in on this, you know, she told herself; after all, the Greybeast got him where it failed with you.

But why Ed?

Why Ed?

Making sure her coat was buttoned to the throat, she slipped outside and waited, letting the cold work on her until she was sure she would handle it. Then she began to walk back to the hidden drive, stopped at the rear bumper and with a second thought, opened the trunk to see if she could find herself some kind of weapon. The thought of it was abhorrent, but there was nothing else for it; if she was stupid enough to want to foray on her own, she was not all that stupid that she would do it without defense.

The dim light buried in the trunk lid was less than useless as she rummaged through the junk she had piled in here over the years, always planning to clean it all out and never quite able to bring herself to it. Finally, with a dry grunt of disgust, she unscrewed the butterfly nut that fastened down the tire wrench rod, hefted it with a wry grin and slammed the lid down after unearthing a flashlight.

Remembering to keep the light aimed only at a slight angle ahead of her, then, she stepped out more quickly, watching for traps that would turn an ankle, for signs that the narrow path's entrance was rigged with warning devices. She found nothing, however, once she had reached the spot, and with a last look at the car she vanished into the woods.

Walking.

Trying not to whistle, trying not to hear the empty sound of her footsteps.

With detached curiosity she noted that the path was barely wide enough for a single car, that once off the Pike and beyond the thickets' wall there were ruts worn into the ground to mark a long time of passage. What grass there was had been stained dark with dripping oil, or had been scorched by the heat of a waiting, patient engine. There was no fence that she could see when she darted the flashlight up and to one side every ten or so paces, nor was there a ubiquitous New England stone wall.

There was no wind.

Nothing moved except her.

And in moving—and resisting the urge to move faster—she wondered why Kraylin had issued his dinner invitation. She almost laughed. No matter what foolish things he and her family had done, Kraylin was no fool in his estimation of her: He knew how he repulsed her, and she was sure that each of their meetings had been orchestrated by him to reinforce that impression. Had he presented his card on a solid gold tray, he knew she would have taken it, and later shredded it with pleasure. The invitation was for show only, so he could report to her mother that the gesture had been made, but please don't be too disappointed when she does not show up.

At that moment she would have given half of her shop and all of her stock to have an instant picture camera for a record of his expression, the look on his face when she knocked on his door.

The path began to veer to the right; several puddles from the last rain were still in the hollows, but sheathed now in thin ice that threw back her light in segmented fires. She began to look ahead for some hints of habitation, saw none and frowned, and hoped her walk wouldn't be long. Her shoes were adequate, but no more than that; had she been thinking instead of scheming, using her head instead of her heart, she would have stopped at the house to change into her jeans and the boots. As it was, stiff weeds and dead branches scraped along her coat, every so often slipping under the hem to dig at her legs. Reflex made her kick out each time it happened, until she realized that she was doing it too often, it was making her tired.

She walked.

And the cold settled tautly on chin, cheeks, ears, nape—drawing the skin tight in preparation for chapping. It crept beneath her collar to work on her spine, wrapped about her joints to slow and to prick her. The coat grew heavy. The collar she had raised to protect what it could seemed to have sprouted needles that rubbed her skin raw. Her hair felt like straw, though she did not touch it; her lips felt like cardboard, as though a lick would send them bleeding.

She knew that much of the discomfort that attacked her now was suggestive—her mind telling her how she should feel, and she felt it, whether it was true or not. She knew this was so, but she could not help the lengthening of her stride, growing careless of the traps that the dark had set for her. The flashlight began to swing with her arm, and she spent less time watching where her feet could fall silent, more time staring through the woods up ahead.

Time became elastic.

She tried counting seconds by thousands, by the beat of her walking, finally admitting she had no idea how long she had been gone from the Pike.

Her teeth began chattering.

Once, as she entered a switchback portion of the path, she thought she heard wings hovering above her; and the flashlight lanced upward, dying before it could reach the first star.

But there was no moon; or none that she could see.

Yet something was slowly giving light to the forest, so slowly she did not notice until she'd stumbled, fallen, the flashlight jarred from her hand and extinguished against a rock. Then there were the trees, vague and disturbing, real and not real as they took on death's pallor. Shadows moved without wind, things rustled without movement . . . things . . . without movement; shadows . . . without wind. Things, and shadows, until she grabbed frantically for the flashlight and shook it until it glowed. Then she knelt on her haunches and sobbed her relief.

*. . . worked for Dr. Kraylin, out on the Pike.*

*Who?*

*. . . worked for Dr. Kraylin . . .*

*Who?*

*Never asked if I heard of it. Just asked me if he worked there.*

The path ended so abruptly Cyd didn't realize she was out of the trees for nearly a full minute. Suddenly the weight of a clearing, the weight of the sky pressed down and alarmed her. Without thinking she snapped off the light and stood there dumbly, feeling as if she had just stepped out of the ocean onto an island, an island where the state of Connecticut should have been.

She was standing on a lawn that, in the afterglow of the light, was a brilliant spring green, too green for the month and the cold in the air. She had an impression of a garden off to her left, another to her right at the edge of the woodland, and an impression she knew had to be wrong that there were flowers still blooming, blossoms that should have been done by the end of the summer. A step forward, and she slipped, dropped to one knee and rubbed at her shin—a stump, and she cursed, stared through the faint moonglow, it had just topped the trees, and saw the lawn dotted with others just as low. Her eyes watered with her squinting, the tears warm on her cheeks, and she let them run for a few moments before taking her sleeve to them.

Another minute of crouching, of waiting, of feeling the cold, and directly ahead formed the vague shape of a building—low, a single story, flat-roofed and clapboard. From where she knelt she couldn't make out a porch, steps or a window. But when she rose and moved several yards to her left she could see the haze of a light spilling onto the grass at the back; and the house was far larger than the bulk it gained from the moon.

"Good Lord," she whispered.

And again caution warned her to head back to the road, to Ed or the police, not to try this alone.

And again was her rage at the lying and condescension.

She pushed the flashlight into her pocket and hurried over the grass, angling away from the near corner of the building, trying to stay in the shadows of the trees that surrounded. As she did, she passed by one of the gardens and nearly stopped in her surprise—she'd been right, there were blossoms, though she didn't know their names. She touched at one as she passed it, drew her hand back at the cold, not bothering to attempt a speculation of the impossible. It was here; she saw it; for the moment it would have to do.

Even, then, with the back wall of the building, she began to move toward it, her ears straining through the silence for the sounds of discovery, her eyes pushing at the darkness to drive it away. Her head began a throbbing. Her left hand started to ache. The minor scratches on her leg began to grow in slow fire.

The corner. She pressed against the wall, peered around to the light and saw a window that stretched from floor to ceiling and was at least fifteen feet from one side to the other. On the lawn were shadow figures, two of them pacing, elongated, grotesque, and she could not help staring until, finally, she shook herself violently and told herself to move.

Gretel returns to the wicked witch's place, she thought as she lowered herself into a crouch and eased up to the sill. And Hansel sits home with a damned bandage on his head.

It was her nerves that made her giddy, made her think in nursery rhymes; but she was grateful for the madness because it kept her from running.

Caution doubly excited. There were no drapes, no curtains, no blinds on this window, and from the angle she could see into the house she spotted the two men: Kraylin, and a shadow. The single light in the vast room—she assumed it made up most of the building—came from a lamp not five feet from her hand, as though it had been encased in clear glass and would glow there forever.

She dropped lower.

Kraylin and the shadow moved into shadow.

She looked behind her, to either side, waited a bit longer before raising her gaze to the level of the sill.

There were three hospital gurneys set head-on against the far wall. On them she could make out the forms of three people covered with white sheets. Two of them were too dim for her to identify, but the third . . .

Kraylin turned and stepped out of the shadow.

# FOURTEEN

Cyd scrambled away so quickly, fell against the house so hard, she was positive the noise could be heard all the way into the village. But there was no sign of immediate pursuit, no cry of discovery as she leaned against the winter-cold wood and tried to find the air to fill her lungs. Her left hand ached, and it was several moments before she looked down and realized she was still gripping the tire wrench so tightly a cramp began to stir at the top of her wrist. She forced herself to relax, to let the iron hang limply in her fingers, and soon enough the pain eased.

An afterimage remained:

The room was nearly twenty feet deep, easily twice that long. The interior walls were fashioned of rough-hewn stone, the ceiling the same with squared and thick posts in its center to support the weight. The flooring was pegged and bare, with islands of scuff marks in the midst of gleaming polish. The single standing lamp by the window had been made of brass, she thought, with a shade of some dark red material from which hung a similarly tinted fringe. She tried to hold the image, thought she had seen through the shadows at the far end—the shadows from which Kraylin had emerged—the outline of a door. She could not be sure.

Only the lamp and the gurneys, and Kraylin walking toward them.

He was dressed as he had been when she had first met him, from blazer to white shoes, but there was a new cast now that startled and warned her—the soft edges to his face, the puffs at his cheeks had hardened and sharpened, his shoulders more squared, his stride a bit longer, even some height to add to the illusion.

No, she thought; it was not illusion. On the outside, past the house and the trees was where the pretense began. That was the illusion. Here was the unmistakable air of immense authority. Here, no matter the outward signs, was a man who was used to absolute control.

She waited a few minutes, debating whether or not to run for her car, decided that as long as she had made it this far there would be no sense in leaving without learning something. With the tire iron, then, still firmly in hand she crept back around the side of the house and peered in the window, wishing suddenly there were some means of overhearing what was said.

Kraylin, beyond the strong tinted glow of the lamp, was standing by one of the gurneys. Carefully, as though he were peeling back skin, he pulled one of the sheets off from left to right and let it hang to the floor. He leaned over, whispered something, straightened and held out his hand. Cyd held her breath, released it in a sigh of knowledge unwanted when Myrtle swung her legs over the side and allowed Kraylin to assist her in standing. They spoke, and as they did Cyd tried to locate any signs of medical equipment, found none and was only a little surprised. Waited to see if the other two would move, scowled when the doctor led her mother away from the wall and toward the lamp, gesturing as he did so to whoever was still standing in the shadows at the room's far right.

Cyd decided as she ducked back away from the window that to continue to watch the mime would be something less than useless. She needed words, not gesticulations, reasons for her mother submitting as she had—and as had the rest of her family, she had no doubt, though which of them remained on the gurneys was still unsolved. She also wanted a reason for her own curious involvement, and to learn this she needed words. Voices.

But there were no windows as she made her way swiftly, quietly, around to the front. And there was no door, no windows facing the path. She swung the tire iron impatiently, ignoring the small stings when it struck the back of her leg. She had to get in somehow, she thought, and when she reached the house's far side she was confident enough to step boldly around the corner, expecting that this wall would be the same as the others.

It was.

But there was also a smaller building fifty yards toward the woods. A garage with doors opened. And in it she could see the face of the Greybeast.

The tire iron fell from her grip, clattering on a stone with a cannon-shot explosion. She snatched it up again, held it tightly like a shield against demons.

She gaped at the limousine, unable to move until somewhere beyond her shock she heard the creak of a door being opened. She turned quickly, saw a shadow push out from the wall, and she ran.

Back across the lawn, dodging the unnatural flowerbeds, gasping at the ice-air that sharpened blades in her lungs. The moon darkened, a turbulence of clouds speeding over its face, and Cyd found herself ducking in and out of thickets trying to find the path. Looking back over her shoulder for those who would chase her. Finally locating the break and, not caring now if she were seen, more worried about her footing, snatching out her flashlight to show her the way.

Shadows. And things.

She had seen it often enough in films and had never quite believed it—that branches and rocks and weeds and twigs could reach out to trip her, snag her, entrap her. That the ruts in the path could widen and swallow. That the air itself could thicken to slow her down while the tears of her racing could blind her enough to send her stumbling into bushes, careening off boles, lose the path entirely and send her thrashing through the shrubs. She cried out when the clouds had done their veiling, and the moonlight created chasms where burrows had been. She leapt over nothings, felt her legs lacerated by whips, heard in the silence the clap of her footsteps, and the hissing of her breath.

Behind her . . . there was nothing.

She tripped, fell, rolled, righted. The flashlight smashed out, but she knew she was on the Pike, spun to her right and raced for the car. Flung open the door and threw herself in, wanting desperately to lie on the front seat panting, shivering, waiting for sunrise to show her the world. But she dared not hesitate, gave in to her own goading and fumbled the keys out of her pocket. The ignition did not fire the first two tries—three times the charmer, she whispered silently to herself. Grinned when it was.

Grinned wider when the car showered gravel behind it, fishtailed and straightened when it bit into the tarmac.

A car passing in the other direction flicked its lights at her. She almost panicked before realizing she had not turned on her own.

When she turned on the radio there was nothing but static.

Abe. She would head directly for the police station as she should have done from the start and lay it all on Stockton's desk and force him into action. It would be simple enough: there's a doctor on the Pike, Abe, who lives about a mile or so off the road in this house that is supposed to be a clinic, but hardly anyone has ever heard of it and he's doing something to my parents because I saw my mother there tonight and . . . well, yes, she looked all right to me, but I'll bet you a million dollars he's got them drugged or something and can make them do whatever he wants, and that's why there's no money. And poor old Angus probably knew about it and was just hoping for . . . oh, how the hell should I know? He's dead now, Abe, and you can't ask him anymore. But you've got to get out there because they want me to do something and I don't know what it is except that they tried to run me down with a limousine and set fire to my shop and—

No. Not if she didn't want to be locked away before she finished.

Ed. It would have to be Ed. She would have to waken him from whatever the doctors at the hospital had given him, tell him the latest and find out what he thought she should do now. But that, too, was useless—if he were still in the same mood as he had been that afternoon, then he would urge her more than ever to give it up before she got hurt, that her father would soon enough explain what was going on and she should learn to trust him just a little bit more, that he's known for years what he was doing and there's no good reason to suspect that he did not know now.

No. Not if she didn't want to kill him before he was finished.

Something thumped from the back seat onto the floorboards.

What she was doing, she realized, was trying to find someone to take the burden from her. That finally her confusion had overwhelmed her, and she was praying for someone else to drink from the cup. But it was her decision. It was her move. Until she had something concrete to bring either to Abe or to Ed she would have to continue on alone.

The rustling of paper.

There was very little satisfaction, grim or otherwise, in the realization that her first impression of Cal Kraylin had been correct, that she had been wrong in dismissing him simply because he had been obvious. The nose on your face, she thought sardonically; the damned nose on your face.

Rustling.

What she would do, then, is return to the house and make a few calls. To Iris, to see if everything went well at the store—and see if she and Paul were at least unharmed; to Sandy, to see if he would work a full day tomorrow and Monday as well, if his parents would let him; to Ed, just to hear the sound of his voice so she would know there was still some sanity in the world, that she was not paranoiac, that she was not simply creating ghosts from the wind that began buffeting the car.

She pulled into the drive without lowering her speed, paying no attention to the indignant blare of a horn whose car she had cut off when she swung across the road. There was no sense of narrow escape, no sense of guilt, only a—

Rustling.

Her foot slipped off the accelerator, her hands dug into the wheel. Slowly, she raised her eyes to the rearview mirror, expecting to see a hand crawling over the seat's back.

Rustling. Paper.

The car drifted to a stop just inside the oval.

Cyd refused to turn around. Her arms were too stiff to move, her stomach and chest too tight for her to breathe, and an ache began to make its way coldly across her forehead as her lips worked for a sound that could turn into a scream. She stared at her left hand, willing it, ordering it, saw it stretch away from the wheel to the headlight knob, saw and did not feel her fingers grip it and turn it to switch on the domelight.

Rustling of paper, and a faint breathing sound.

The tire iron was on the seat beside her. She grabbed it, lost it, grabbed it again, and in one swift motion opened the car door and twisted around on the seat, the iron rod lifted to smash what she saw.

On the floorboard.

Her arm trembled.

The crow had been wrapped in a dish towel, had been stuffed into a brown paper bag. But the bag was now writhing, bulging, *rustling*, as the crow tried to work its way out. The crow that had attacked her . . . the crow that was dead.

She felt nothing as she raised herself higher on the seat, felt nothing at all as the tire iron smashed down onto the bag—once, twice, a dozen times over.

"You're dead," she whispered harshly.

The bag still moved.

Once, twice, a dozen times over.

"Damnit, you're dead!"

And the bag still moved.

The iron slipped from her grasp and fell out to the ground. She pushed herself out of the car and kicked the door shut, checking numbly the windows to see that they were closed. Then she stumbled backward away from the car, shaking her head, her lips still working though the words would not come. It was impossible, of course, she told herself shrilly, and it was only the light of the moon that made the paper seem to move. But when she looked up at the sky, the moon was gone, the clouds overcoming it in waves of deeper black. She tripped, then, over the raised bricks at the oval, landed on her back and allowed herself to scream.

And scream.

And cry. Until she felt pebbles beneath her digging into her spine and she rolled to her knees and stared at the car. Tried to tell herself immediately that she did not see the shadow that darted helplessly inside, slamming against the glass, connecting once with the horn and shattering the air. There was nothing inside. There was nothing at all.

Only the pain in her knees and the numbness in her arm, and the sandpaper rasping that tore at her throat.

She rocked back to her heels, looked down at her palms and felt more than saw the dirt and stone there. Something to do; it was something to do, she thought as she rose and walked slowly toward the house; and she fished the handkerchief from her pocket and daubed at her hands, was still working to clean herself when she opened the front door and turned on the foyer light. Winced when she saw the dirt stains on the cloth, was about to stuff it back into the coat when she realized with a frown that the handkerchief wasn't hers.

The camel's-hair coat. Ed. The night she had found the death certificate in her pocket she had also taken out . . .

She stumbled across the floor to the staircase, sat heavily and gripped the bannister with her right hand.

There was dirt on the handkerchief, but there was no blood.

A single-winged bird had tried to kill her.

Her father had been dead, and was living again.

The death certificate had not been some macabre, unpleasant joke; it had been a preparation in case something had failed.

Angus had told her of a mild heart condition that Kraylin had treated, and had treated well. Now Angus was dead . . . or was he dead again?

Cyd laughed. She leaned back on her elbows and let the stairwell fill with her voice, let her voice fill the house, let the house echo it back by the tens, by the thousands, denying and crying and demanding the dream end.

"Oh my God," she whispered.

*People die; Yarrows don't.*

She threw the handkerchief from her, watched it flutter to the floor and assume a vague tent shape. She ran, then, to every room on the first floor, turning on every lamp until the house was afire and the shadows were gone and a wind of false warmth followed in her wake. Dying as soon as she reached the library, dying when she looked in spite of herself at the floor behind the door where the dead crow had landed.

There was no blood.

Her coat felt unclean, as though it were leprous and she shed it as she began running again, up the stairs this time and into her room. There was no question now that she had to get to Ed, had to fall into his arms so he could raise his battle shield. It made no difference now that he was afraid; he had been right from the beginning—she should have gotten out. She had no time to pack, however, only time enough to grab a coat from the wardrobe in her bedroom, notice that it was the green one, the one the bird had torn.

She dropped it where she stood.

Frowned.

Knelt, and reached into the pocket, finding there the note she had taken from Rob's desk. Her fingers would not listen to what she commanded, and the paper dropped twice before she could unfold it. In green ink, in a hand precise as it was bold, there was a single message across the center: *You'd better be ready. He does not respond.* There was no date, but she knew it had to have been the twenty-third of June; there was no signature, but she knew it was Kraylin's writing; and there was no salutation. To whom had it been written, then? Not necessarily to Rob; there'd been dust in the desk when she'd finally prized it open, and anyone could have hidden it there if they knew he scarcely used it.

Rob. Evan. Mother.

"I'm crazy," she muttered as she got back to her feet. "I'm crazy and I don't know it. That's the way it always is."

She wandered out into the hallway and stood at the head of the stairs. The lights notwithstanding, she felt herself poised in the center of a vast well of darkness through which lightning, subdued, flashed on occasion, illuminating nothing but her reflection on the black. There was a core of intelligence in this well that had given her the answers, the thread by which nearly everything could be bound; but she refused to accept it, refused to draw it, could not believe that there were powers within the Station that defied what she had known were consistently immutable.

What she had known.

She had *known* that birds with one wing could not fly; she had *known* that once cut with a jagged shard of glass her mother would bleed; she had *known* that her father had lain dead in his bedroom; and she had *known* that she had placed a dead crow in a towel, in a bag, and had been forced to beat it with a tire iron in the car.

What she had known.

One step at a time she descended the staircase, her left hand gliding along the bannister without gripping, her right clutching in spasms at the buttons on her blouse. She felt her shoes sink into the carpet, heard the soft press of her heels and the give of the leather. The wind outside was a distant moaning thing, lost among the lights that guided her down, without the power to harm her, to touch her, to blow away sanity and leave her with . . .

As she grabbed onto the newel-post with both hands and squeezed as though she could crush the polished wood, she decided to rid herself of fantasy before it was too late. To deny everything in the face of what she had seen, what she had found, would only tend to make tornados of her confusions and drive her into cellars of madness and warmth. To flow was the answer, to speculate and refute.

Assume, then, she told herself, that the bird was indeed dead, that her father was indeed dead, that her mother did not bleed—assume it for the moment without a single scream. Assume that this insanity was engendered by Doctor Kraylin—through hypnosis (don't ask yourself how the dead can be affected) or drugs or a combination of both. Assume further, and rightly, that the family had been in minor financial trouble before she herself had left on her tour of Europe; that was an open secret, there could be no argument there. Then Kraylin had convinced one, two, however many of the Yarrows that whatever he did was worth the price that he asked, the price that included a handful of lives.

Angus. Wallace. Father. Perhaps . . . Mother.

Her brothers were left, then.

Unless they were dead, too.

She grinned without mirth: the stumbling block to belief was not the supernatural. More things, Horatio, and the rest of the misquote—she would believe in anything if it could be proven beyond doubt. The stumbling block lay in the fact of her own life, that for the last three months she had been living with the dead. That she would not tolerate, that she would not accept.

Consider, however, a part of her whispered—wouldn't that account for the changes you saw? Your father without his blustering; Mother's sudden fear of doctors; the *indifference* you've wept over since the day you got off the plane; Angus' abrupt turnabout and the hiding of truth; the dismissal of the Lennons and Wallace McLeod?

And that *something* you sensed each time you came home?

Could not it have been the absence of life?

She shook her head vigorously and rushed into the sitting room, to the far side beyond the second fireplace where she flung open the doors of a walnut cabinet. From it she grabbed a bottle of Bourbon, splashed as much as she dared into a tall crystal glass and drank it before she could imagine the burning. And when it came and she gagged, she drank again, and again. Set the glass down and sagged into a chair.

Insane, of course.

The whole idea was gothic: drive the poor little rich girl right out of her mind, settle her portion of the dwindling estate and divide it. Divide it. But division meant partners. Two at the least; at the most . . . *my God!*

"All right, Cyd," she said out loud, "you know damned well there's only one way you're going to convince yourself one way or another."

But she could not get up to go out to the car.

And in facing that fear and the possibilities it bore she knew that in spite of the storm in her mind, in spite of the denials that all science had taught her . . . in spite of it all, she had accepted it all.

There was no need to face the dead crow that lived.

"No," she said, ten minutes later.

"I don't know."

She stood suddenly. This wavering between the real and the unreal would last all night, for the rest of her life if she let it. She needed to verbalize it, to talk aloud to someone who could play the devil's advocate with a modicum of humor without laughing her right out of the room. That, without question, would have to be Ed. No matter the pain, or the drugs that they'd fed him, he would have to hear her; hear her, and now.

She returned upstairs only long enough to yank her cardigan from the wardrobe and kick the green coat under the bed. The note she left lying in the middle of the floor, unafraid but unwilling to touch it again. The handkerchief also remained where it had fallen, and she gave it wide berth as she came down the stairs and headed for the door.

Stopped.

Listened, with one hand on the knob while the other fussed meaninglessly with her hair.

She listened for the sound of the dead crow flying, for the first time realizing that unless she could somehow exorcise the car she would have to walk all the way into town.

And in listening heard the sound of a motor in the drive.

You did it, Ed, she thought with a grin; by God, you did it!

She opened the door and stepped onto the porch. Several seconds passed while she waited for her eyes to adjust to the night; and when they had it was too late to duck back inside.

In the oval, at the curve by the garage, headlights flared out and an engine died.

And all she could do was stare at the Greybeast.

# FIFTEEN

When the driver's door opened she could see five faces inside: Evan, Rob, and her mother in back; Barton and Cal Kraylin seated in front. They were motionless for several long moments, but it was more than sufficient for Cyd to understand that here was the proof of the nightmare she had been feeding. Not that it would stand up to scrutiny in a court, and not that even Ed would believe it unless he saw. Nevertheless it was here. Nevertheless she had it. It was an intuition that leapt into something not quite faith and more than terror; it was the acceptance she had felt inside about the bird, and the knowledge that Horatio should have been here after all. Real and unreal was a problem that had a solution—both real and unreal existed as one. A particle here, an atom there, a shade for this portion . . . all of it of a piece and none of it separate; and none of it meant a damn unless one believed.

And she did.

As Kraylin and the others stepped out on the drive, and Evan and Rob moved immediately to the car and peered inside, Evan shrugging, Rob nodding, as Kraylin and her parents waited by the Greybeast's hood.

Oh Ed, Cyd wept silently, for the last three months I've been living in a tomb.

They stood in the glow of all the house's light and waited until they were once again five. Then Kraylin looked steadily in her direction, as if waiting for her to join them, out of fear or resignation. And when she did not move he nodded, stuffed his hands into his blazer pockets and began to walk toward her, the rest trailing a step behind.

Normal; they look normal, some part of her cried. But the illusion, now that she had pierced it, was not quite complete. Like the tiny brass horse in the library, now that she understood that what she was watching was false, there were minute items missing, items that glared in their absence: the barely military swing of Barton's left arm, the stilted stride of her mother, Evan's birdcock tilt as he seemed to listen to the ground more than air. All of it missing, vital parts so small they were taken for granted and thus overlooked.

Kraylin lifted a hand in a mocking gentle greeting, and she bolted.

She slammed the door and raced down the hall toward the back, skidding on the bare sections of flooring but keeping her balance without losing her speed. At the back door she paused, a panicked look to either side, then flung it open and was ready to sprint across the veranda to the lawn when Evan stumbled around the corner of the house. She stared at him for a moment before doubling back toward the stairs, had her hand on the bannister when she looked up and saw Myrtle on the first switchback landing.

Rob stood in front of the sitting room entrance, and across the foyer waited Barton, his hands clasped at his waist.

Kraylin was at the door, hands still in his pockets, rocking on his heels like a skipper at the helm.

"Are you finished?" he said. The hardness she had seen at the Clinic was still there, a stone-rough edge that gave timbre to his voice to help it carry though he whispered. "Are you finished?"

No, she thought, you murderer.

She nodded.

Kraylin raised his thick brows, seemed to sigh his relief, then indicated with a nod that she should follow her father into the living room. She almost hesitated, changed her mind about running when she heard Evan striding up behind her. She did not turn around; instead, without looking at the others she walked carefully into the room, afraid she would stumble over her own shadow or another's, not willing to give the doctor the satisfaction.

Without waiting, she headed directly for the wing chair that flanked on the left the television hearth. She looked at the blank screen, saw her faint grey reflection, turned and sat and crossed her legs. She would listen, she thought, because it would give her time; time for the improbable to alter definition, time for something positive to come to mind. And when it did she would be ready. Given the chance to run, she knew where she would go.

Kraylin waited on the threshold, his gaze examining the room as if it held a trap before moving deliberately to the divan that was set on her right. He took the far corner, draped an arm over the back, unbuttoned the blazer and rubbed idly at his stomach.

Immediately, Cyd pointed to the four Yarrows arranged behind him. "Get them out of here," she said tightly, amazed that she had not exploded in tears. "I . . . I know what they are. They don't have to be here."

"Well," Kraylin said, his admiration showing. "If you think that will help you, of course." And he lifted one hand in a listless dismissal.

"Can you do that every time?" she asked, wishing she could sound far more calm. When Kraylin nodded she almost spat in his face. "So? Now what?"

Kraylin brushed a hand through his wind-blown hair, as if in a moment he would be sitting for a portrait. He fussed at it, patted it, smoothed it down to his nape, taking so long that she thought she would scream. Then he shifted his attention to the front of his shirt, again patting, again smoothing, until he was satisfied.

"If you wait a minute," she said, "I'll get my purse and give you a nail file."

He did not smile.

"Listen, Doctor," she said, the use of his title as close to an obscenity as she could get, "you can keep on doing what you're doing, or you can threaten to kill me, it really doesn't make a bit of difference to me. You're not frightening me. I'm scared to death already."

He nodded, slouched deeper into the corner and cleared his throat theatrically. "When I was younger," he said, his gaze fixed at some point on the ceiling, "I used to daydream a lot. About being able to control things no one else could. Or make things, like Victor Frankenstein. It's not all that unusual, you know. All kids dream about being magical, fighting monsters, wondering what it would be like to be a vampire or a werewolf—without, of course, any of the pain that goes with them. So I did it, just like everyone else, the difference being that I didn't let go. I read books, I saw movies, sometimes I even promised to sell my soul to the devil in return for some bit or piece of magic for my own.

"Naturally, it didn't work.

"And neither did the nonsense that Mary Shelley wrote about in her novel. Oh, I don't deny that I thought about it once in a while during the time I spent in medical school, and afterward, while I did research in France and England. I thought about it, dismissed it, but I didn't stop dreaming. The best time, as you probably already know, is when you first lie down in bed and your mind isn't quite ready to let go for a bit. It's also about the only time you can control your dreams. You force the action, as it were . . . and so I forced my magic."

Cyd listened carefully, searching for signs of the madman in the voice, finding none and realizing that this made it all the more terrifying. The man was serious. She wished the wind would stop blowing.

"And then, when a little bit of inheritance money drifted my way, I began visiting clairvoyants, mediums, other charlatans of that ilk, thinking that perhaps they had stumbled upon what I had been only dreaming about. I did this, you must understand, only half-heartedly. It was . . . rather like a hobby, I would say. Something to pass the time when there was nothing better to do. I suppose a psychiatrist would call it a fetal obsession, one that feeds on you slowly until it gives birth to a psychosis."

Bingo, she thought; and knew it was too simple.

Kraylin crossed his legs and grabbed hold of his knee. His gaze had shifted, from the ceiling to her breasts, though she could tell that his vision was somewhere else, somewhere inside and he didn't see a thing. Nevertheless, it made her nervous and she turned slightly away.

"I began to feel afraid for myself. But the irony of it is, the more afraid I was that I would drive myself crazy, the more I began to think that maybe, just maybe this magic business had a foundation I could unearth, as it were, and build on if I had the right tools. And the right attitude. And that, my dear Cynthia, was the key to it all.

"Attitude.

"You see, daydreams are one thing and reality is quite something else. You can daydream all you want, but unless you *believe*, not a blessed thing is going to happen. And the reason most people don't believe is because they've been trained not to. One believes in illusion, but not in magic.

"So I worked at it. For several hours every day, for years at a time. I would stand in front of a mirror and tell myself it was true. I would whisper it to myself during an operation—you look surprised, Cynthia. Did you think I was a quack?"

She was startled and angry that she'd allowed something to disturb the carefully built neutrality of her expression. So startled in fact that she nodded without thinking, and shrank back into her chair when Kraylin stiffened and scowled.

"I am a good doctor, Miss Yarrow," he said slowly. "A very good doctor. If there's one thing I'm not, it's a phony practitioner."

"I'm sure," she muttered, flinched again when he struggled to his feet and stood before her.

"I will not be patronized, Miss Yarrow!"

She shook her head quickly. "Not me," she said. "I was just agreeing with what you said. You said you were a good doctor, I said okay."

His chest rose and fell rapidly, and he turned away sharply to face the front windows with his hands behind his back. The drapes there and the shades were drifting slightly as the wind found cracks in the panes and the frames, created draughts that became snakes to creep along the floor. Her ankles grew cold, her calves and her thighs.

"It happened two years ago," Kraylin said, his back still toward her. "One morning, after all that self-promising, I was able . . . I was able to do something! It doesn't matter what. I did it. And it wasn't telekinesis or telepathy or any of that other nonsense about ESP. It was magic, Miss Yarrow. A certain kind of magic."

He spun around, one arm outflung, and she almost yelped and raised her palms toward him.

"It's all right," he said softly. "I don't throw lightning bolts or anything like that. I don't pull rabbits out of hats or create windstorms or fire. I'm getting there, to be sure, and one of these days all those elements will be mine to control. Earth, wind, fire, water. But not yet, Miss Yarrow. Not yet, and I'm patient."

She looked toward the foyer, looked back at Kraylin. You're crazy, she tried to tell him; you're out of your mind.

*Dead crow . . . flying.*

She drew her legs up under her and hugged her knees tightly. Heard footsteps upstairs and frowned until she realized that someone was moving from room to room, following her earlier race, turning out all the lights.

And the wind . . .

"It takes a great deal of concentration," he said, bending forward at the waist as though talking to a child who was a great deal shorter, "and it takes nearly everything I have. You have to be strong, Miss Yarrow. Very strong indeed. And I knew almost at once that I would have to give up my practice and my research if I wanted to keep hold of what I had. But to do that I needed money. A great amount of money. And where better to find it than Oxrun Station."

She swallowed to kill the dryness in her throat. "Where . . . where did you meet my father?"

"Angus Stone," he said without hesitation. "The old man was the first one I'd met when I came here. He had a reputation for fairness, and liking a bit of the greenback for himself now and then. I . . . well, I gave him a demonstration, so to speak. I showed him what I could do, and what I needed so that I could keep on doing it, so I could get stronger. He introduced me to your father."

"And you killed him."

"I can raise the dead, Miss Yarrow."

"You killed him because alive he would have none of your nonsense. He didn't believe you, whatever you told him, so you killed him so you and Angus could get hold of the money."

He took a step toward her.

"Don't come near me," she spat, her feet down to the floor, her hands gripping the armrests as if ready to spring.

"Or what?" he said with a twitch of a grin. "You'll tear out my eyes? Miss Yarrow, I think we had better understand each other a little more clearly." He took a deep breath, held it, released it, moved away from the divan to pace the open floor, though not once did his eyes leave her, measuring her, checking to be sure that she could not outrun him. "I can, literally, raise the dead. That takes concentration. It takes, as I've said, a great deal of power. But once done . . ." He stopped and pointed at her sharply. "Once done, Miss Yarrow, my creations last for hours. Not many at one time, of course. I'm not a juggler. But while they last they do my will. They don't have instructions, not to the letter, because they're not zombies, my dear. They are living creatures of my creation that happen also to be dead."

Cyd wanted then to place her hands over her ears, her eyes, whatever it would take to drive the man from her. It was madness she was hearing, and madness she believed—Father was dead, and Mother did not bleed. They had been murdered in some way—how agonizing to think that it didn't matter how—and Kraylin had retrieved them. Used them. Sold property and valuables to keep himself going—in a manner, she thought through a swirling cloud of hate, that he would like to become accustomed to. And it followed in diabolic logic that the sons would be next.

One question remained, "Why aren't I dead?"

The doctor cocked his head, his eyes narrowing into a concentrated squint that seemed to swallow his face until only his mouth was left.

"I don't need you," he said. He shrugged as though the answer were simple. "I don't need you. The money is mine, and I have proved to myself what I can do. I was prevailed upon not to kill you when you returned, and so I did not."

"Generous."

"Expedient," he corrected. "As I said, I don't need you."

A shadow swelled on the foyer wall, someone waiting just beyond the door.

"But now you will have to kill me, won't you," she said flatly. There was no query; it was a matter of fact.

And she was startled when Kraylin shook his head slowly. "I still have no need," he said. "Besides, my dear Cynthia, who would believe you, eh? No one, that's who, or you would have headed straight for the police, or that . . . boyfriend of yours. You know people will think you're mad, crazy, whatever you choose to call it. No one will believe that you've been living with the dead and not known it."

"The office," she said quickly, a grasp at a straw. "Someone down there will believe me, I know it. Someone would have noticed by now that Father is . . . different." She felt the tears again and fought them. "Someone will know."

"Not quite," he said smugly. "Your family hasn't owned that bank for at least, oh, eight months. It was the first thing I had sold."

"But Angus—" She stopped, closed her eyes briefly, snapped them open again when she heard herself crying, a faint and distant wailing that was building to escape. She had to get out. One minute more in the company of this nightmare and she would lose all hold of what sanity remained. Lose all control . . . Control. "Wait a minute," she said softly. "I thought you said it took a lot of power, or whatever it is, to do this . . . this thing. Then how could you . . ." Her eyes widened.

Kraylin nodded. Again the teacher, this time complimenting on the insight that had been reached.

"Who?" she said. Then she waved her hand to forestall his reply. She knew. It was Evan. Evan in the background for all of his life; Evan who did most of the work and took most of the abuse; Evan who was the middle son and received the dwarf portion of affection once she had been born and there was a girl in the house. Evan who worried about everything night and day, who had less sleep than anyone until a solution had been found, a buyer put off, a poor risk unloaded. Evan whose loyalty was to the fortune, not the family.

"How did you convince him to murder his own parents and his brother?"

"I showed him what to do."

"You mean, he can . . . ?"

"You almost said it just a moment ago, Cynthia. To make this work so no one would know, I had to have someone else working with me. The sorcerer's apprentice, so to speak. When I couldn't be here, he kept the charade going."

The fight was gone. The rage was gone. There was only the numbing advance of despair. In a situation so totally intolerable, the only saving grace had been the thought that all of them were dead, all of them trapped in a hellish limbo of this man's creation, and none but herself, by virtue of her absence, had escaped. But now . . . but now . . . that Evan had actually, of his own free will, of his own damning choice, deliberately become a partner to the demon that stood before her—it was too much. There was too much weight for her shoulders to bear, too much was being asked of her now, too much . . . too much.

She knew she had slumped, but she did not care. It would be vain, it would be more than self-destruction to keep the pretense of defiance now.

That one of her own had actually *chosen* to be with him!

Evan spared you, remember. You could have been dead.

Dead.

Peace.

Darkness.

She wanted it.

What was the sense? she wondered. To fight against something that could not be defeated, to struggle against a tide like the Canute of legend? Why bother? What in God's name was worth standing up to the man who stood triumphantly before her, hands folded at his waist like some fiendlike priest awaiting the acolyte who brings him the chalice?

And the worst of it was, he would continue to spare her. Whether she moved out of the Station, or stayed in a place of her own in the village, she still would *know*, and the knowing and the helplessness would soon drive her to a grave she would dig with her own hands. First would be the death of her mind and its attendants, slipping deeper into the peace that silence would bring her, ignoring the world because the world would be changed; then aging, slowly or rapidly as her dementia dictated, to be buried in the Park with the rest of the living.

A telephone rang.

Kraylin hurried to the foyer and made a quick signal, and she saw the shadow billow and shrink as whoever had been waiting went into the other room. A voice. Soft. Calm. Immensely aristocratic. A moment later the doctor returned.

"That was Mrs. Lennon," he said, as though it did not matter. "You'll be pleased to know that today was your best day. I told her you would bring champagne when you came in."

"I wish I had the vocabulary to call you what you deserve."

He held up a forefinger in admonition. "Cynthia, that's hardly the way to talk. You'd think I was a megalomaniac, determined to raise all the dead of the world and take it over, as if they were some kind of a private army. Ah, you're surprised! I'm ashamed of you. I'm not greedy, Miss Yarrow. I know what my limitations are, and I know that it will take me many years before I could even begin to be that strong. No, my dear, all I'm after is the knowledge. To know that I can do will be reward enough.

"It's as your brother said: 'What a hell of a thing, to have your daydreams come true.'"

She expected him then to break into a high-pitched cackle, to run his hands gleefully at the thought of his success. Instead, he only shrugged; and in that swift movement, in that one small reaction, she saw the strain that worked on his face. The sharp edges, the hardness, the alteration of his features were not, as she had imagined, the result of playacting. He was straining. He was trying to speak normally with her while at the same time retain control of his . . . things. And things is what they were; they were no longer her family.

Strain.

And weakness.

And Iris and Paul and Ed and Sandy and Yarrow's on Centre Street where people bought their . . . dreams.

She almost laughed, and it was a struggle not to; she nearly leapt from her chair, gripped the armrests to prevent it. What despair there was had vanished in the instant.

Myrtle and Barton and Rob . . . Angus and Wallace and a helpless black crow.

They were dead and wanted burying, and she would be damned first to give Kraylin the last call of mourning.

She stared at him, seeing in his subtly altered expression a sense of her decision. He returned her gaze, only his hands moving to betray the unease he was working with, the sudden realization that Cyd was now his enemy, and an active one at that. She knew he was wondering what had gone wrong with his presentation; and presentation it was, of that she didn't doubt. Every word that he said, every move that he made had been calculated to drive her into that blinding despair. That it nearly worked served to chill her, made her wary when he turned and called for her brother.

And when he stepped into the living room, his smile almost rueful, she was not surprised that she had been wrong once again.

"Was it really so bad? The business, I mean. Was it all that bad that you had to do . . . this? With him?" She rose and moved to stand behind the chair, her hands on the back and gripping it hard.

"Bad enough," Rob said. "Not to mention the fact that we were never all that accepted here, and you know that as well as I. The Station is old money, Cyd, and we're not. Not yet."

Angus had said he'd given the shop's papers to Barton and Rob; on the night of the opening Rob had cut his hand and bled; and the note in her pocket had been written to Rob, who had, for once in his life, panicked and had filled out the death certificate in case cover had to be created for a failure of Kraylin's.

Robert the eldest, who would not die poor and would not die weak. She wondered if the doctor knew him as well as she did.

He seemed to know what she was thinking. With a quick, jerking motion he strode away to the windows and watched the shrubs battle the wind. Cyd took the opportunity to come out from behind the chair, a careful eye on Kraylin's uncertainty as he tried to keep brother and sister in sight at the same time.

"Now what?" she said.

"I saved your life," Rob said without turning around. "Just go away, Cyd, before you force me."

"Oh really," she answered, the sarcasm as heavy as she dared make it. "Well, I suppose I should thank you, shouldn't I? Thank you for taking away my family, and thank you for ruining me for the rest of my life—or did you think I'd be able to continue living, here or anywhere else, knowing what I do about this obscene thing you've done?" She took a step closer to the foyer door, a single step closer to Kraylin by the divan. "Oh, and I forgot: thanks for sparing Ed. I imagine it was you who was driving that car all the time. Nice work, brother. I wish you'd killed me."

Rob looked at her then, malice and anguish a pair in his eyes. "Cyd—"

"I would tell you to go to hell, Robert Yarrow, but it wouldn't do any good, would it."

"All right, Miss Yarrow," Kraylin said quickly. He moved toward her, his hands outstretched as though to restrain her, his eyes darting from side to side as he realized that somehow he had lost his control.

Cyd didn't wait for the rest of his admonition. She lunged toward him, but not at him, her right arm lashing out with all her strength at the shoulder; and the flat of her hand slashed across his throat. He spun away from the blow, grappling for air, caught hold of the back of the divan and fell, heavily, onto the floor.

Rob yelled.

And Cyd ran for the door.

# SIXTEEN

The front door was locked, and Cyd wasted no fruitless time in tugging and kicking. Immediately she saw that exit was barred she pushed herself away and sprinted into the sitting room. Heard movement behind her, unhurried, unworried, and the thought that her recapture was so foregone to them fueled the rekindling of her dormant rage. With one arm she swept a lamp and ash tray from a small end table, grabbed hold of a leg and in one spinning motion punched the table's surface through the nearest window. Again; again; setting her back to the sill when she heard her name shouted, listening to the faint silvered sounds of the glass landing on the ground, the walk, the blacktop beyond. Feeling the wind kicking into the house, instantly lifting all drapes, curtains, shades with its hands, all table cloths and fringes and chair aprons and clothes. Another lamp tipped over, shattered and went dark, the sparks of its dying caught in the air and whirled into nothing. The scent of rain. The scent of fear.

Kraylin and Rob stood in the doorway while Evan advanced on her one step at a time. Behind them she could see her mother and father standing in the foyer, oddly slumped as if marionettes with one string missing.

"Come on, Cyd," Evan said. He reached out a hand; it trembled. Kraylin had one hand clenched to his throat.

"Get away from me," she said, and brandished the table.

Evan smiled. "Come on, Cyd, let's stop this, huh? Father's going to kill you for that window, you know."

He was less than three feet away and tensing to lunge when she beat him to it, thrusting with all her strength and releasing the table, at the same time spinning around and throwing herself outside. Trying not to cry out—the last thing she had seen before leaving the floor was Evan, his hands still groping after her while one table leg jammed into his cheek, tearing it, pushing it back toward his ear . . . and he was still groping as though he hadn't felt a thing.

The shrubs broke her fall. Branches and needles whipped at her arms, her face, the exposed flesh of her legs. She rolled, came to her feet and, with a last glance at the window, scrambled along the walk until she could run upright, ignoring the blood that ran down her calves, knocking away with a fist the threat of blurred vision. She had thought to make for the trees in back, clamber over the wall and lose herself in the forest. But that would do her no good now, not with Rob knowing the trails as well as she, not without a purpose as she struggled over the hills.

There was Ed, however, and she had to reach him. No matter how he felt, what condition he was in she had to reach him, to be safe for a while.

The front door slammed open; light spilled like white fire to the walk and the drive.

A shout. She did not turn. Ran faster until she had reached the car, saw the tire iron in the shadows and grabbed it with both hands. The metal was cold, and she relished its burning, held it in front of her protectively as she yanked open the door and jumped to one side—and a thing not a bird darted out, and fell: a mass of black feathers that writhed on the ground. Grimacing, she kicked it away, could not help looking up to the house . . . and freezing.

On the walk stood her parents, and Evan with his face torn apart. And on the stoop Kraylin struggled with Rob. The doctor was shouting something incoherent, his voice so harsh she could feel the pain. Rob was impervious. He looked down at the short man, his face darkened in anger, and with a single almost careless swipe of his arm sent the man reeling into the corner of the wall that protruded from the door. From where she stood she could hear the sickening crack of skull against stone, could see Kraylin's eyes widen in shock and disbelief before he staggered forward, stumbled, fell into the shrubs, with one hand clawing uselessly at the leaf-covered concrete. Clawing, stiffening, reaching . . . still.

"Cyd!"

Despite the warnings that stormed through her, she took a

step toward him as the wind keened over the roof, sent leaves out to blind her. The cold was raw.

"Cyd, you know I can't let you do this!"

Her tears were as much from her sorrow as her rage, and there was nothing more that she wanted now than to plant the iron in his heart and tear it out again. Her grip tightened. Her legs trembled. She stepped onto the drive, her head up and slightly tilted against the direction of the wind.

Rob glanced down at Kraylin, then glared out at her and lifted his fists to the level of his brow. The glare deepened. Cords of muscle sprang up at his neck, drew back his lips until the glare became feral. A damp leaf plastered itself against the center of his chest. Another. And another, while rivers of the same poured in through the doorway, and the mouth of the broken pane.

"You can't do it," she said steadily, not loudly, but sure. "The sorcerer's apprentice nearly got himself killed."

He could not be shaken; he could not hear her. The veins across his brows and the backs of his hands rose and pulsated while he worked on his teaching; and Cyd frowned, wondering, for her parents and Evan had not moved from their spot. Then what—

She heard it before she saw it.

Turned.

The Greybeast snapped its headlights on . . . one at a time. And the noise she had heard was the tires moving over the leaves; the engine was still, and still the car moved. From the mouth of the drive slowly toward her. Slowly, less slowly, as the grille caught the houselight and seemed to snarl at her, the headlights only bright enough to give them mocking life.

She backed away.

Less than fifty yards.

Looked back over her shoulder and saw her family waiting. Three dead, and waiting; one living, and hating.

Rob grunted and thrust his arms upward as if lightning were prowling for the word of his command, as if thunder and fire were stalking his direction.

He can't do it, she thought as she backed toward Barton; if Kraylin hadn't the time, and the strength for this magic, then

Rob was in the act of taking something he couldn't handle. And at that moment she knew the only way she could survive.

And she almost balked when she turned to face her mother, her father, the poor accused brother.

No.

Not Mother. Not Father. Not Brother.

They were dead.

She spun around to face the Greybeast, saw it lurch into a speed it could not have achieved normally, and she only imagined the growling of the engine as it took the oval widely and bore down upon her. Bore down, glaring, the reflection of the houselight blurring the windshield, reminding her and frightening her, turning her legs to stone . . .

. . . as she lifted her arm defiantly and flung out the iron, heard as she leapt screaming it spear the grinning grille.

Saw the Greybeast lift as its front tires hit the bricks, lift and leap and soar and snarl, toppling Barton and Myrtle and Evan beneath the chassis, at the last moment hanging there several feet off the ground as Rob stared at it unbelieving, master and master, knowing and knowing, while the wind keen turned to screaming and the beast's fender caught Rob's chest, smashed him aside and plunged through the door.

There was silence in the wind.

With Cynthia, weeping.

Later standing and moving, one thing left to do.

And the funeral was held on a bright and blue Monday. Most of Oxrun had turned out at the Memorial Park's service, and most of them were proud, and frankly amazed, at how well the younger Yarrow bore up under the strain. Three coffins at once in three adjoining graves, and her eyes were as dry as were most of theirs. So they passed their condolences and their smiles and their kisses, and they donated flowers in wreaths and bouquets. And avoided the figures on the far side of the gravesite—the two solemn policemen and the man in the wheelchair.

Ed held her arm loosely, and she patted his hand whenever she could, whenever she dared, feeling her cheeks ache at the smile that she kept there, feeling her eyes ache at the tears already shed. It had been two weeks since the nightmare at the house, but she had insisted that Rob be able to attend. It would kill him, she'd told the police and the judges, if he could not be there with her to watch the family buried. There was no real way of knowing, of course, just why he had done it, but she told Abe Stockton that the business was in trouble, that the bank had been sold and the money was going quickly. Despair, she guessed under Ed's hard and unbelieving stare, and just like him to think that honor was best served by the honorable way out. In the city they would call it a suicide pact, and a reporter that Marc Clayton had placed on the story had guessed in his article that the smashing of the house and the grey limousine was somehow symbolic of the failure of empires.

Cyd never took issue. She only planted the ideas and let others grow them. She only waited until Rob was well enough to attend, then forced him to watch as the coffins were lowered. The only thing was, he would probably never understand. When he had been struck by the car, his head had hit the wall . . . and now, in the daylight under the winter-warm sun, he only stared uncomprehending as the mourners filed away.

"Cyd," Ed whispered, "I think it's time for us to go. Do you want to . . ." and he nodded toward the policemen who were wheeling Rob away.

"No," she said. "He wouldn't hear me anyway."

"Do . . . do you want me to leave you alone for a while?"

She gripped his hand tightly, so tightly she knew it hurt. "Please, no. I've already done all I can."

The Lennons approached them then, with Sandy behind. Iris was still weeping, and Paul was too straight, but Sandy was fiercely calm and held out his hand.

"I . . ." He stopped as Iris took light hold of his arm. "We're sorry, Miss Yarrow. I don't know what to say."

"It's all right, Sandy," she said, not brave enough to keep one tear from escaping. "I just don't know how to thank you."

"Could get into the store on time for a change," Iris muttered through her crying; and the laughter Cyd heard then was amazingly her own—the laughter and the tears and the holding of old friends until she was alone again with Ed and walking slowly over the grass.

She was worried about him, but would not let her worry and her grief make her change her mind. His own accident had made him too weak to run his own business, and she was finally making progress in getting him to see a doctor. But she dared not move in with him as he had already suggested. That would be a mistake in more ways than one—primarily letting him think that she would accept his proposal. But not now, not while the nightmare was still clinging to her sleep and she was still working on the life she had been building before it happened.

At the gates to the Park, then, they stood awkwardly together, watching as the policemen waited with Rob at the curb, waited while an ambulance made a slow U-turn to pull up in front of them.

"Cyd—"

Her car was standing not ten yards away.

"Ed, we've already been over this."

"I know, I know. I'm sorry."

"Now listen to me, you idiot," she said, turning full toward him, her hands on his chest, one fussing with his tie. "You promised me you would see a doctor, all right? You promised me, Ed. Those black-outs aren't funny, and you're not a superman."

"Damnit, they'll go away if I'm careful."

"Sure they will, and trees will learn to walk. Confound it, Ed, am I going to have to postpone—"

He held up his hands in easy surrender. "No, no, don't be silly. You go ahead and take that trip. You need it. And I promise you that I will see Doc Foster the first thing in the morning. And if he wants to put me into the hospital, I'll do it. All right? Does that make you happy?"

She smiled and shook her head slowly. "You need a baby-sitter, you know that, don't you?"

"I know what I need," he said.

Attendants moved at their own pace from the ambulance, one of them lighting a cigarette for a cop. With Rob between them they chatted, and laughed, until one of the patrolmen looked over to Cyd and winced his embarrassment.

Cyd tried to steer the talk away from his proposal, suddenly remembered a gift in the car. She told Ed to wait and hurried to the car, reached in through the open window and pulled out the saber that had hung on her brother's wall. It was polished now and gleaming, with a garish red bow tied at the hilt. She saw the police staring in frank admiration, saw one of the attendants take Rob's chair and push it toward the back.

"No," Ed said, backing away.

"Yes," she insisted, and handed it to him, poking at him with it until, reluctantly, he grabbed hold of the blade. "You've loved this thing for years, and you might as well have it. I've sold just about everything out of the house, and the realtor says he may have a buyer for the place and the land." She stared blindly at the sunlight glinting off the hilt. "I don't want anything left, Ed. I don't want anything left at all."

She released it suddenly, as though it had burned her. Ed grabbed for the hilt before it struck the ground, gripping the blade tighter, then cursing loudly as he dropped it. She bent, but he waved her away, wiping his hand on his coat gingerly.

"Damn, woman," he said, "you want to call me lefty from now on?"

She grabbed at his wrist and turned the hand over. There was a deep crease across the palm.

"I'm fine," he said. "Stop fussing."

The ambulance pulled slowly away from the curb.

"Damnit, Cyd, what's the matter with you?"

The skin had been broken.

"Cyd?"

She watched, turning, the ambulance pick up speed. Her brother's face was in the back window.

"Cyd, listen, I just want you to know that I'll be waiting for you when you get back. I know it sounds like something Sandy would say, but damnit I love you, and I'll be waiting when you get back."

On Ed's hand there was no blood . . .

"Cyd, I'll be waiting."

. . . and Rob was smiling.

After selling almost forty short stories, and six novels, Charles L. Grant decided to give up his teaching career, and become a full-time writer. He is twice the recipient of the Nebula Award, given by the Science Fiction Writers of America, first for Best Short Story, and most recently, for Best Novelette. In addition, Mr. Grant has been published in *Analog, Fantasy and Science Fiction, Midnight Sun, Shayol,* and anthologies such as Orbit, Year's Best Horror, Nebula Awards, the Arts and Beyond, Future Pastimes, etc.

THE LAST CALL OF MOURNING is the third novel set in Oxrun Station, a small New England town where strange and supernatural events occur. The previous novels, THE HOUR OF THE OXRUN DEAD and THE SOUND OF MIDNIGHT have both been nominated for the Best Novel in the Annual World Fantasy Awards.